TANGLED TRAILS

**Center Point
Large Print**

**This Large Print Book carries the
Seal of Approval of N.A.V.H.**

TANGLED TRAILS

Jim Kane

CENTER POINT PUBLISHING
THORNDIKE, MAINE

This Center Point Large Print edition
is published in the year 2009 by
arrangement with Golden West Literary Agency.

The text of this Large Print edition is unabridged.
In other aspects, this book may vary
from the original edition.
Printed in the United States of America.
Set in 16-point Times New Roman type.

ISBN: 978-1-60285-463-5

Library of Congress Cataloging-in-Publication Data

Kane, Jim, 1913–1983.
  Tangled trails / Jim Kane.
      p. cm.
  ISBN 978-1-60285-463-5 (library binding : alk. paper)
  1. Large type books. I. Title.
  PS3505.O6646T36 2009
  813′.6—dc22
  2008054987

09-1229
Golden West
(Center Point)
5/09
29.95

This book dedicated to
my father-in-law . . . . .
Percéval Garant.

CHAPTER ONE

— "Bat With a Colt" —

"Dangest-lookin' cat I ever saw," Tully said, putting a hand to his partner's shoulder to steady himself. He pressed his nose against the clean glass of the show window, just under the neat black lettering which read: CURIO SHOPPE.

"Little cuss's grinnin' at us!" he marveled. "Lookit, Slim!" He hiccuped loudly, wiped his mouth with the back of his sleeve and looked up at his partner with drunken solemnity. "What say we take the pussy back to camp with us?"

Both men were new riders with the Open A, having joined the outfit at Cottonwood, two hundred miles inland. The Open A was starting a cattle drive to the Gulf port and had found itself short-handed. Tully and Slim had hired on.

Now, the drive over and the cattle safely in their loading pens, they had seen the sights of Lafitte, sampled its liquor and its women, and, busted but happy, were on their way to join the rest of the outfit camped on French Creek seven miles out of town.

That was when Tully spotted the cat in the window.

Tully climbed unsteadily to his feet and pulled

Slim up behind him. They headed for the door and went inside.

A bell tinkled softly somewhere in the back of the shop. They stood in the dim quiet, two bedraggled range hands trying to keep a straight stance. Old armor looked down at them from the walls where hung ancient firearms, dueling pistols, swords, and clocks by the dozen.

A girl finally appeared on the short flight of steps leading to living quarters behind the store. She hesitated on the last step, eyeing them doubtfully.

Tully nudged Slim as he swept his battered Stetson from his head. Slim followed his gallant gesture.

"Afternoon, miss." Tully's voice was slightly blurred. "We've come for the cat."

"Oh!" The girl came toward them with quick steps. She was small and dark and piquant. A fragrance, as of lilacs, came with her, dispelling the faint smell of mustiness in the shop.

"Mister Hegstrom sent you? No?"

Slim blinked at Tully, who nodded with solemn gravity.

Slim was beyond the point of rational conversation. His glazed eyes sought out the object in the show window. The small ebony cat sat on a pedestal among tinted glassware and bone-carved trinkets. A bit of glazed pottery, it was seated with its tail curved around its hind legs, both paws frozen in the act of wiping its tiny nose. It was jet black except for its eyes, which were of green Mexican jade. There was nothing unusual about the bit of pottery except for its smile; a smile that seemed to express a secret, ironic pleasure.

Slim reached up and scratched his thinning brown hair over his right ear. "Reminds me of Wong Foo," he mumbled. Tully's weight was beginning to tilt him off balance.

" 'S'right," Tully agreed. "Grins jest like cookie." He was shorter than his lanky companion by a foot, broader and more voluble. "Lesh give it to the Chink. Might be good for an extra hunk of pie, come chow time."

Slim stepped back from the show window for a long range view of the cat. Without his support, Tully lost his balance. He flung his arms out for Slim, and one hand hooked into the lanky puncher's coat. Slim wrapped an arm protectively around his companion, and they both sat down hard on the plank walk.

Tully wagged his head. "You shouldn'ta pushed me, Slim." He was facing the street, looking up into the sad brown eyes of his cayuse, which was nosing the short rail beside Slim's mount. Between the two animals lay the cobbles of Orleans Avenue, and the alleyway directly across gave him a glimpse of the sea.

This was Lafitte, the first port town Tully and

Slim had ever visited. Both men were inlanders —this was their initial glimpse of a body of water they couldn't "spit across." "Yeah—Mister Hegstrom sent us." To Tully's knowledge their hard-fisted trail boss didn't even know the black cat existed. But if this girl wanted to think Myles Hegstrom had sent them to pick up the cat, why disappoint her?

The girl turned to the show window. She reached inside, plucked the tiny statuette from its pedestal and went behind the counter with it. She wrapped it swiftly in heavy brown paper.

"Five dollars, please."

Tully dug into his pockets and stared blankly at the three one-dollar bills in his hand. He turned to Slim. "You heard the gal," he mumbled. "Shell out!"

Slim emptied his pockets. With his silver they made up the five dollars.

The girl said worriedly: "Take good care of it, *messieurs.*"

Tully bowed. He had trouble focusing his gaze on the girl. She kept changing into twins, both small and dark and anxious. "We'll take good care of it," he promised gravely. "Feed it every night." He turned to Slim. "Won't we?"

Slim nodded. "Nothin' 'll be too good for Wong Foo's cat," he promised.

The girl watched them stagger outside, and only then did a small suspicion nudge its way

10

into her head. Those two men—*mon dieu!*—they were drunk! Mister Hegstrom would not have sent two such men for the cat!

A chill went down her back. At any moment her stepmother would return. And Therese Monet had been coldly definite concerning the disposition of that statuette!

She ran to the door. But the two punchers had already ridden around the corner and disappeared. She sank against the door framing, fear forming a cold lump in the pit of her stomach. Those men had not been sent by Myles Hegstrom at all. . . .

Slim and Tully rode out of town with the westering sun dimming under an off sea haze. Trail boss Myles Hegstrom had been blunt about leaving in the morning, and it was close to sundown now.

They rode steadily, heading in the general dirtion of the Open A camp. The haze thickened and the wind that blew against their necks turned chill. Daylight faded swiftly, and as the chill grew sharper they stopped often for swigs from the bottle they had taken with them. With the last drink they lost all sense of direction.

An early moon stained the haze with an orange glow. The wind picked up, shredding the high mist, allowing fitful glimpses of the gibbous satellite. On the Gulf horizon lightning ran its forked tongue across black, boiling clouds.

Half asleep in the saddle, Tully and Slim were unaware of the brewing storm. The animals had settled down to a slow, aimless drifting across the grass flats.

Slim roused himself once to peer into the night. "There's the crick," he mumbled. "But where's the chuck wagon?"

Tully lifted his head and tried to focus on the dark line of foliage ahead. 'Darn fools prob'bly drifted . . ." His chin sank back against his chest. "Might as well make camp here . . . find them . . . in the morning. . . ." His voice trailed off sleepily.

Slim nodded agreement. The animals had halted at the edge of what seemed a natural fording. Ahead of them the water slid with a pale sheen, about a hundred feet wide at that point and less than stirrup deep.

Some vague impulse stirred Slim. "Might as well cross here." His low mutter didn't reach Tully, who was already snoring, but Tully's rawboned grey horse followed Slim's animal as it splashed across the creek.

They pulled up under a tall pecan tree that sifted the hazy moonlight into a dappled pattern under it.

Slim slid wearily out of his saddle, uncoiled his rope and secured his rangy roan buckskin to a young sapling. His mind was in low gear, and only the deep-worn grooves of habit dictated his moves. He came back to the animal and loosened its saddle cinches, letting saddle and underblanket fall at his feet. The mare snorted tiredly and moved away.

Slim scratched his head. He was facing the creek as he did this, and he caught a glimpse of a shadow moving swiftly against the skyline. Something black billowed out behind the prowler, like some monstrous wing.

He blinked, rubbed his eyes and peered into the darkness. Tully was still in the saddle, drowsing over his gray's neck.

"Tully!" Slim whispered. "Wake up! We're bein' followed by a spook!"

Tully raised his head with an obvious effort. He tried to focus his attention on his partner. "Seein' things again," he deprecated. "Last time it was pink gila monsters. Dang it, Slim—yo're drunk!"

Slim shook his head. Uneasiness was working its way through the fogs of alcohol. He slipped his Colt free from his holster. "I think I'll take a look-see down by the creek. Never did like spooks—"

He stumbled off into the darkness. Tully grunted and fell asleep again.

Slim walked to the edge of the creek and stopped with his boots in the water. He squinted across the stream, hearing nothing but the soft fretting of the current and the rising mutter of the wind.

He brought his Colt up and absently rubbed his nose with the muzzle. "Reckon I am seein' things," he muttered. He started to turn back when his ears picked up the swish of boots coming through the water.

His reactions were slow. He swung back to meet the sound and had time to glimpse a bat-like figure appear out of the shadows; to catch the dim flick of light from a long blade in the man's lunging hand!

Slim's left hand went across his chest in a vain effort to shield his body. His right hand jerked up, his fingers tightening convulsively against his trigger. Both movements were frantic and ineffective.

The slim blade went completely through him, just under his shirt pocket. Slim's mouth popped open, but no yell emerged from his suddenly constricted throat muscles.

The blast from Slim's Colt awakened Tully. The racking explosion jerked him upright and nearly unseated him. His gray mare pranced sideways, eyes rolling.

Tully grabbed for his Colt. He kneed his animal around to face the creek, alarm driving the sleepiness from him.

"Slim!" he called anxiously.

He saw shadows move by the creek, and then

the moon spilled its revealing light through a break in the driving scud. Twenty feet away a batlike figure froze. . . .

Tully never saw the man clearly. He fired once, hastily. The jarring explosion billowed smoke up into his face.

The prowler's first bullet ripped into his stomach, just above the belt line. It knocked Tully back, driving his breath from him. A searing fire spread through his guts. He dropped his Colt and clawed for his saddle horn.

The mare was dancing sideways. The second shot from the creek burned a shallow gash across its lean flank and smashed Tully's kneecap. The sharp pain lifted the animal in a twisting turn just as Tully's clawing fingers dug into its thick mane. Self-preservation pulled the dying Open A puncher forward to bury his face in the coarse mane hair.

The third shot from the cursing man by the creek missed altogether as the clouds came together again, blotting out man and animal under the pecan tree.

The gray mare lunged away, with Tully clinging like a burr to its neck. . . .

Several miles north of French Creek Luke Riatt crested a low, yucca-spotted sand hill and pulled up to measure the oncoming storm. Luke was a big man in his Texas saddle, braced against the quick running wind. The animal he rode was big; it had to be to carry the solid weight of the man. A rangy black, sleek-muscled, powerful, it sniffed the wind with flaring nostrils.

They had come out of the empty land behind them, drifting toward the coast. Now the big Ranger leaned forward, surveying the pale flats below. He had cold, gray-green eyes, this Texas lawman . . . tiger green, flecked with black. And there was something of a big cat's wild assurance as he probed the empty land below the hill.

Texas born, he had left that state after the war, the sour taste of defeat still rankling. He had been twenty then, and although Lee had surrendered at Appomattox, Luke had not bowed to the inevitable nor waited through the ugly period of Reconstruction. He had drifted north into Wyoming, married and taken root, only to have his wife and young son taken away from him by cholera two years later. Alone again, and bitter, he had drifted once more . . . eventually returning to Texas and a job as civilian scout for the Army. From there it was a natural step into the only Texas organization that provided law and order in those turbulent and savage years . . . the Texas Rangers.

But the loss of his wife and child had left its deep stamp on him. . . . Essentially a lonely man now, he was given lonely assignments. Tough, durable, and unimpeachably honest, the name of Luke Riatt carried a harsh and fearful connotation beyond the borders of the Lone Star State. . . . It was a reputation well founded.

He was on assignment now, on a job a little out of the scope of his experience and in a section of Texas unfamiliar to him. He had never been to any of the Gulf towns. He was an inlander, born and bred, and the salt tang of the sea was something he did not know. Nor did he know the ways of seafaring men.

Now he studied the horizon, his eyes narrowing and cold. Lightning forked through the black, piling clouds. Thunder muttered on the wind that flowed against his hard face, bringing the smell of rain with it. His big dun horse snorted and shook his head, jingling harness.

Luke smiled. There was the unfamiliar salt tang of the sea in that wild-running wind, and he guessed he was not far from the port town of Lafitte. Again he judged the wind and the play of lightning on the horizon and knew that the storm would beat him to Lafitte.

He was turning for his slicker when his big dun snorted again and pointed into the wind. The big Ranger turned his hawk gaze to the flats below him.

The thin haze running before the storm did not entirely blot out the moon. Out of the distance on his right Luke saw the rider—a dark blob clinging to the back of a gray mare racing across the grass flats.

The Ranger's eyes narrowed. "Looks like someone's in trouble, feller," he muttered to the dun. The stallion leaped forward at the touch of his heels.

The mare veered away as the big dun appeared on its flank. The dun stretched its stride, rapidly closing the distance between them. A hundred yards beyond Luke reached out and caught the gray's bit reins.

"Whoa!" he commanded sharply.

Fear had spent itself in the mare, and she came willingly now, easing to a trembling stop. Riatt turned his attention to the man hunched over the saddle horn. The rider was lifting his face from the mare's long neck hair. He had lost his hat, and the top of his bald head gleamed in the pale light. His round face was a pasty gray, pinched tight around his mouth.

His right hand clawed at his empty holster, kept fumbling there as though there were no connection between the futile gesture and his brain. In the pale moonglow Luke spotted the blood glistening on his saddle, darkening the man's coat front.

"Easy, feller!" the big Ranger muttered. He dismounted quickly and eased the man down, propping Tully's head in the curve of his arm. He didn't have to look further to know that this man would be dead in the next few moments.

Tully's pain-filmed eyes focused on Luke's face. He couldn't see clearly, but what he saw eased him. This was not the man who had shot him.

"What happened?" Luke's voice was gentle. "Run into trouble?"

Tully tried twice before he got a whisper out. "Bat—with—a Colt. Danged spook . . . must have killed . . . Slim. Down by the creek. . . ." A tremor wracked him. His voice faded, as if he were suddenly very tired. "Cat . . . in my saddle bag. Yores . . . stranger . . . take good care . . ."

The wind ruffled the dead man's fringe hair as Riatt eased him down. The man's words made little sense. Bat with a Colt! And a cat in his saddle bag! What in the devil was he doing with a cat in his saddle bag?

The Ranger turned to the drooping-headed mare. He didn't find the kind of cat he expected. He found a neatly wrapped package instead. Frowning, he tore it open, and the wind took the paper from his hands and whirled it away.

The black cat's jade green eyes caught the moon's rays just before the first dark tendrils of the storm clouds hid them. The eyes seemed to wink up at the big Ranger.

Luke turned the statuette over in his hands, shook it. It appeared to be solid. But it was just a figurine, a plaster image of a cat made to decorate a mantelpiece. Nothing unusual about it, except for its half secret, half sassy smile.

But the dead man's last thoughts had been with the cat. Was this small piece of glazed pottery the reason he had been killed?

Thoughtfully Riatt slipped the cat into his saddle bag. The gray mare sighed heavily. Turning to her, Luke noticed the long shallow gash across her flank.

"No wonder you were scared," he muttered. He ran his hand along the mare's neck, his frowning gaze lifting past the animal to the darkening land. The dead man had mentioned a partner named Slim. . . .

He turned to his big dun stallion. "Let's go take a look," he suggested coldly.

CHAPTER TWO

— The Angry Man —

There was no trail visible to the ordinary eye, but Luke Riatt backtracked Tully's mare with a sureness born out of an ingrained sense of observation. He had a mental picture of the direction from which the gray had appeared, and he knew that an animal, hurt and frightened, generally ran in a straight line unless turned by natural barriers.

Dark cloud masses were blotting out the moon as he neared French Creek. The brush line made a darker outline against the horizon, broken by clumps of upreaching shadows that were trees. That was all—but the big Ranger knew he had come to water.

His hands drifted down to the butt of his holstered gun, riding snug in the holster. He glanced back to the gray following docilely enough on his lead rope. Tully's body was draped across his saddle.

Ahead of the Ranger a tall pecan tree thrust its dark shape against the sky. The shadows were black under the tree. A horse whinnied eagerly in the darkness, and Tully's animal snorted a greeting, tugging suddenly at her rope.

Luke eased his dun toward the sound. The wind shook the pecan tree, rustling through the leaves. A dark shape moved against the blackness, and shod hoofs pounded against soft earth.

Luke slid alertly out of the saddle, a gun in his fist. Slim's buckskin whinnied tiredly as he came up, jerking at its stakeout rope. The Ranger touched the animal's flank, turned and stumbled over Slim's saddle. He hunkered down, his eyes becoming accustomed to the deeper shadows, and ran his hand over the saddle. What he didn't see he felt. The saddle bags had been opened and searched!

He turned his head toward the creek. There was no sound in the night. The wind came from the sea, rising and whipping through the brush. Luke straightened and headed for the creek. He moved slowly, like some wary jungle animal coming to a waterhole. His boots touched something soft, and he crouched, his narrowed eyes making out the dark shape of a body lying face down in the shallows.

Grim-faced, the Ranger pulled the man out of the water and brought him back to the dubious shelter of the pecan tree.

The big dun stood still against the darkness, but Tully's gray mare shivered and whinnied questioningly. The Ranger knelt beside the body and struck a match, shielding the tiny flame with his hat.

The creek water had washed away most of the blood. He had to look closely to find the puncture in Slim's shirt.

Riatt frowned. The match curled and died, and the shadows closed down on him. The man across the gray's saddle had been killed with a .45 slug. But this man had been killed with a sword—a rapier rather than a sabre!

The first rain sifted through the leaves, spraying the motionless Ranger. He felt the chill against the back of his neck, but he didn't move. He remained crouched like some grim carnivore, his green-black eyes remote, his thoughts slipping back to Ranger headquarters, to Captain Hughes' frowning face as he had introduced Luke to a heavy, serious-faced man seated by his desk.

"Luke Riatt, Joseph Russell, head of the State Customs Office."

Russell had a strong handshake. "Heard a lot about you, Luke. Mostly from John here."

Luke had waited, wondering what was bothering the Customs Department. Captain Hughes answered him. "Joe's been having trouble, Luke. He's lost two men in the past two months in Lafitte, a tough port town on the Gulf."

Russell nodded. "Usually we handle our own troubles. But right now I'm short-handed. I can't spare another man to ride down to Lafitte to ferret out what happened down there."

"Smuggling?"

"I think so," Russell added heavily. "Bert Morse went down there on a routine check. In less than a week he was dead, stabbed to death in a fight over a woman!"

The Customs Chief made an impatient gesture. "I received the report of his death from the town constable, a man who signed himself G. Jenkins. The report was later confirmed by the deputy sheriff who made an investigation. Jenkins' report had stated that Bert Morse got involved with an entertainer in a gambling house and had been killed by a jealous suitor named Enrico. Enrico was later killed while resisting arrest. The deputy sheriff's report bore out the town constable's statement."

Russell shook his head. "I wasn't satisfied. I sent Carl Drake to check up on Morse. I received one report from him. It didn't mention Bert at all. He wanted information—a description of the late Empress Carlotta's jewels. I answered him in care of the Pierre House where he was staying."

The customs chief stopped pacing. "This same G. Jenkins replied a week later. Drake's body had been found in this same entertainer's bedroom. His official conclusion was that Drake had been stabbed to death by an unknown assailant. Motive, jealousy."

Luke's smile was humorless. "Did he mention the entertainer by name?"

"Lolita." Russell frowned. "That's why I don't go along with that town constable's findings, Luke. Bert Morse was—well, he might have played around. He was young enough to feel his oats. And he wasn't married. But Carl Drake had a wife and two children in Galveston. I'm not saying that's enough for every man—but it was enough for Carl Drake. I've known Carl for years, and I'd stake my life on it. If he was up in this girl's room, he wasn't there for play! He found out something—something Bert Morse had run into and been killed for!"

"The Empress Carlotta's jewels?" Luke had mused. "A dozen stories have come out of Mexico about those jewels—the only valuables the Empress tried to save from Maximilian's colonial venture."

The rain began to tear through the shielding leaves, bringing Luke's thoughts back to the body at his feet. A killer with a sword—Carlotta's jewels—and a black cat with jade green eyes!

Somewhere in Lafitte he expected to find the answer to all three. . . .

The southeaster lashed Lafitte, driving men indoors, leaving old cobbled streets empty. Wind made a wild cry above the rain, high over the port town that had been Spanish, then French, and now was Texan.

25

Lafitte was an old town—a town of brick and masonry dwellings, of narrow streets and wrought-iron gates; a place where laughter and tears were hidden behind closed shutters —where dinner was served by candlelight in small walled gardens away from the streets.

Most of the town was crowded on the rocky bluffs above Spanish Cove, and it took the squall with stolid indifference. The cove waters were comparatively quiet. Two miles from the bluffs a narrow sand island made a natural breakwater. In daytime the ruins of an old fort, rumored to have been built by the pirate Lafitte, were visible from the bluffs. A man with glasses could make out the four-foot-thick walls that enclosed a square, two-decker masonry building; could spot the rusting six-pound cannon still in their emplacements, facing the sea.

Inside the protection of the cove, the schooner, *Port of Call*, rolled easily, its sails furled and made fast against the blow.

The girl came out of the blackness of a narrow side street, pausing to press her slim body against the building side. She was not dressed for the weather. She had on a simple pink cotton dress, high-collared and not new, and a pair of high-buttoned gray shoes not made for hurrying.

She glanced back into the darkness, knowing that she had little time to waste. Her right cheek was bruised, and the back of a hard hand had split her lower lip. Defiance had rammed color into her cheeks, and it was still there. This time she was never going back!

She pulled her black silk shawl up to shield her face from the rain and looked up and down Orleans Avenue. Light from the windows of the tavern across the street fell weakly on the gleaming cobblestones.

No one was in sight. She took a long shuddering breath and started across. She heard the rider as she was halfway over, and fear spurred her. Her heel caught in a crack between the pacing blocks and her foot twisted sharply. Pain stabbed up from her ankle, bringing an unwilling cry from her lips. Her foot gave beneath her weight and she fell, sobbing as much from fright as with pain.

Iron-shod hoofs rang sharply in the night. She tried to crawl across the street to the protection of the shadows beyond.

The black horse loomed up in the rain, rawboned and wet and snorting softly. She turned her head, the rain pelting her white face. She saw the man slip out of the black's saddle and bend over her.

"You hurt?" There was concern in his voice.

She sat up, feeling embarrassed and confused. The rain had soaked through to her skin, plastering her light dress to her small, well-curved

27

figure. She pulled the shawl around her in a futile gesture of protection.

"I think I sprained my ankle."

The man slid a hand under her legs, the other about her shoulders, and lifted her. He was not a big man, but he seemed to pick her up without much effort. Close to, she saw his face in the diffuse, rain-misted night. It was a young, darkly handsome face, smooth-shaven and finely chiseled. He smelled clean.

"I'll take you home, miss."

"No!" The girl's voice held panic. "Not home, *monsieur!*"

The stranger's lips pulled out in a thin smile. "To the doctor, then?"

The girl shook her head. She turned to look back along the empty street, and her eyes were dark and expectant. "Turn left at the next corner if you wish to help me, *monsieur.* There is a boarding house—Madame Couet's—"

The young man's voice held a dry humor. "Bad night for one of the Madame's girls to be out, isn't it?"

The girl colored. "Madame Couet is not what you think, *monsieur.* She is—" She took a deep breath. "It does not matter. Please—if you wish to help me!"

The man nodded. He lifted her up to the black's saddle, eased up behind her. His right arm went around her trim waist, and her softness brought a gleam to his eyes. She stiffened, her body erect in saddle.

He smiled. "I'm Remington Drake," he said gently. "What's your name?"

He felt her quiver. Her face turned to him, and he saw the bruise on her cheek, and it took the indolence from him.

"Drake?" she whispered. "I knew a Drake—" The young man's eyes were suddenly cold. "I'm Carl Drake's brother!"

She nodded slowly, turning her face away. "I'm Justine," she said. He barely caught her name, her voice was so low. "My stepmother runs the Curio Shoppe three blocks down the street."

He said stiffly: "I came past it on my way in. Are you sure you don't want to go home? I can turn back—"

"No! No!" Her voice held desperation. "I never want to go back! Never! If he doesn't get the black cat back he'll kill me! He said so!"

Remington Drake's arm tightened about her waist. "Who'll kill you?"

But the girl only buried her face in her hands.

The rain battered them as Drake turned his black horse left at the corner, as he had been directed, and rode down a dark street that had no sidewalks. Ahead and on his left Madame Couet's sign gleamed wetly in the light of a hurricane lamp hung on a nail. The boarding house was a boxlike building with a door and two

29

windows fronting the muddy street. The door, a solid, double-paneled oak barrier, was at street level; the two windows, green shutters closed against the storm, were on the second floor.

Drake halted the black before the closed door. The girl said, "Many thanks, *Monsieur* Drake," and started to slide down from the saddle. The man's arm tightened about her.

"My friends call me Rem," he said. "I like Justine."

She didn't smile. "I must go now," she protested.

"Wait. I'll help you inside."

She shook her head. "No. I will manage. You must go away from me. If they have followed me—if they see you with me—they will kill you, like they killed your brother."

Remington Drake slid uncomfortably out of his saddle. He was a slender man, just above medium height. His expensively cut suit was soaked. A black leather Gladstone bag rode on his saddle cantle. Either he did not mind the weather, Justine decided, or he preferred the discomfort of getting wet to the bother of buttoning up in a slicker.

He reached his hands up for her, and she looked down into his face. He was a polished gentleman with a nice smile. But the impression faded as she felt the hard presence of a gun under his coat.

He set her down gently. "That's what I came to Lafitte for," he said ambiguously. "I think I'll come inside with you, Justine. I want to know exactly what happened to my brother."

She was turned to him, her back against the door. Her eyes were big and black against the bruised whiteness of her face.

"It would do no good," she whispered. "The first one—the blond man named Morse—he found out about the black cat. He came in to buy it. He was killed. But he must have told your brother. Carl came into the shop later; he wanted to know about the cat, too."

The black horse suddenly shied, and the girl's eyes jerked past Drake. He saw fear distort her features. Her mouth opened. But Drake didn't hear her cry out.

He was turning when a huge fist smashed against the back of his head. He fell against the girl. That much he was aware of, before the night rushed him into the deep pit of unconsciousness.

Justine finally screamed, once. Then the big black man, his naked torso gleaming in the flickering light of the hurricane lamp, smothered her cry with a big palm. He lifted her as if he were handling a doll and turned to the small man standing a few paces away.

"Take her back home, Etienne!" the man ordered. He was an old man, in his sixties, but he stood erect under the lash of the rain. A black cloak, heavy from exposure to the storm, hung from his narrow shoulders.

The big black nodded. He was an enormous-muscled man, looming a full head and a half over the girl. A knife scar puckered the muscles of his broad back but did not seem to handicap their functioning. He took his palm from her mouth, and the cloaked man said: "You will go willingly now, Justine?" His voice was soft, but there was no mercy in it.

The girl nodded dumbly. She did not look down at the man sprawled at her feet.

The old man lifted a silver-knobbed walking stick and pointed it at Remington Drake. "Who is he? What did he want?"

"I don't know," the girl answered. The lie came easy. "I fell while crossing the street. I think I've sprained my ankle. He rode by, stopped to help. That is all I know."

"We'll see," the cloaked man said. He made a gesture with his walking stick, and the big black took the girl's arm and headed her back toward Orleans Avenue. The old man waited a moment longer. The young man sprawled before the door of Madame Couet's was beginning to stir.

Perhaps Justine had told him the truth. He and Etienne had come out of the alley in time to see the man lift her from the street. If so—

His hand toyed with the silver knob of his stick.

Above him a window grated open. A woman's muffled voice was whipped by the wind. The old man hesitated, then faded back into the blackness of the night.

The shutters of the windows directly overhead were pushed open and a middle-aged, graying woman looked down into the street. She mumbled something uncomplimentary, then lifted her voice to someone in the room behind her. "Just some drunk who fell off his horse, madame."

She closed the shutters and brought the window sash down. In the rain the big black horse waited patiently for the man stirring in the mud at its feet. . . .

Luke Riatt came into Lafitte with the bodies of Tully and Slim across the wet saddles of their horses. He came in along the cove road, feeling the full buffeting of the rain squall. The lowing of Open A cattle in their pens off the dock, coming in snatches on the capricious wind, brought a frown to his face.

The big dun's hoofs rang on the slick cobbles of Orleans Avenue. It was late and the wide street was almost deserted. Most of the store windows were dark, their windows shuttered against the storm. Several taverns spilled a dim and futile light through their steamy windows. A buckboard was tied to the hitching post in front of one of these establishments.

Small crooked alleys angled off from Orleans Avenue, leading down to the waterfront. Lafitte was an old town, even older than the State of Texas, and its history was linked to the sea. It looked different and it smelled different from the raw jerry-built prairie cow towns. The veneer of two cultures, Spanish and French, had been brushed over this port town, and it wore its years like a woman—the signs of age were there, but how old Lafitte was remained its own secret.

There were few places in the Lone Star State that Luke Riatt had not visited. But Lafitte was new to the big Ranger. He knew something of its history, which was inextricably mixed with legend. Legend had it that Jean Lafitte, the pirate, had once run his ship aground on the sand island protecting the cove and had become intrigued with its possibilities as a hideout. He had built a fort on the sand spit which later became known as Buccaneer Spit, and when things had gotten too hot for him in New Orleans, he had spent some time in Spanish Cove.

Lafitte, it was said, had been initially settled by men of the pirate's crew who, tiring of the hazardous life, took to the more peaceful pursuit of fishing for a living.

That much Luke knew of the town's past. Its present was still unsavory. It had a reputation as a tough port town. Killers with a price on their head drifted into Lafitte to pick up passage to South America, and seamen of a dozen different nationalities often jumped ship here, preferring the comparative freedom of the waterfront dives to the hard-fisted driving of their ship's captain.

But Orleans Avenue, Lafitte's main thoroughfare, was quiet and deserted as Luke Raitt rode over the glistening cobbles. He let the stallion pick its own pace, while his hard glance searched the building line for the law office. The Ranger had on his hands two dead men whom he wanted to turn over to the proper authority.

Despite the protection of his slicker, rain had seeped down his neck, soaking the shirt around his shoulders. Sitting a wet saddle didn't improve his disposition. He had come a long day's ride, preferring to push the dun to make Lafitte by night, and he had not expected to be delayed by the two dead men behind him.

Rain sheeted across the road, drumming against Luke's face. He closed his eyes momentarily, ducking his head against the pelting drops; when he looked up again the rider was in the road in front of him. Apparently he had just emerged from a narrow side street and pulled up in the middle of Orleans Avenue to get his bearings.

He was only a vague figure atop a big, thick-chested black horse when the Ranger first noticed him. Riding close, Luke saw that he was a slender young man with a gray Stetson sitting back jauntily on his head. His well-cut town clothes had evidently been exposed to the weather for some time, and there was mud on his pants.

Some drunk too far gone to worry about the rain, Luke thought sourly. He eased his dun stallion to the left, intending to cut around the rider.

The big black jumped forward at the press of Remington Drake's knees, blocking Riatt's horse. The dun snorted, tossing his head impatiently.

Luke leaned forward on his saddle horn. His voice was tart. "You know where you're headed, mister?"

Remington Drake, still a bit groggy from the blow he had received, straightened quickly, his Colt in his hand. "Sure," he said bitterly. "Do you?"

Riatt settled back in his saddle. The youngster's face was tight, and there was a reckless gleam in his eyes. There was something riding this man, Luke thought grimly. He wasn't drunk. . . .

Raw impatience edged Luke's voice. "It's no night to sit here and argue that point," he growled. "Put that gun away and let me by!"

Drake underestimated the big man facing

36

him. He was hurt and soaked and his pride needed to be restored; he wanted to vent his anger on something tangible. And this big man with two burdened horses trailing behind would do for a beginning.

"I seldom argue," he sneered. "Don't feel I have to, with this gun in my hand." His glance flicked to the bodies draped across wet saddles behind Luke. "You the undertaker here?"

"No." Luke's voice was short. He didn't relish sitting there in the driving rain, and temper roughened his voice. "I just work for him." He pulled his dun to the left, making another attempt to pass.

Young Drake blocked him. "We'll quit playing guessing games, big feller." His voice was ugly. "Where is she? The girl from the Curio Shoppe?"

Riatt's heels raked his horse's flanks. The big stallion acted on cue. He lunged ahead, hitting the black horse with his shoulder, almost knocking the animal off its feet.

The Ranger's left hand chopped down on Drake's wrist, sending his Colt clattering to the cobbles. His right fist whipped around and collided with Drake's jaw.

The man went backward and slid out of the saddle to fall in a loose-muscled sprawl in a shallow puddle. He didn't move.

Riatt massaged his bruised knuckles. "Guess

you were drunk after all," he muttered. "The rain ought to sober you up some."

He had half a mind to leave Drake lying in the puddle. But something in Drake's lean young face, upturned to the pelting rain, touched a soft spot in the hard-jawed Ranger. He dismounted and caught the weary black's trailing reins before the animal could wheel away. Holding the horse with his left hand, Luke bent and clamped his right hand around Drake's belt buckle. He lifted the youngster off the cobbles, carried him like a meal sack to the scant protection of a darkened doorway and left him there with the black's reins looped to the nearby awning support. He went back for the youngster's gun, hefted its balance and shrugged. He skidded it across the road to the huddled figure.

Then he turned to his dun horse, which was waiting patiently. "Let's get in out of this rain," he growled, "before some other darn fool starts asking questions."

Two long blocks up the avenue a board sign, creaking on corroded hinges, caught his eye. "The Pierre House—Rooms by the day or week."

The name rang a bell, and then Luke remembered that Joseph Russell had said that Carl Drake had put up there. It was a three-story stone masonry building wedged in between a dark pastry shop and a wide alleyway. Someone had block-lettered the word "Stables" in black paint on the hotel wall, and a reasonable facsimile of a hand pointed down the alley.

Luke turned into the empty rack in front of the hotel. A small archway in the masonry wall sheltered a heavy wooden door, closed against the storm. He opened it and found himself facing a poorly lighted narrow room with a small bar on its left and a flight of stairs on his right. Under the stair landing was the hotel desk and the mail pigeonholes.

Two customers lounged against the brass rail —burly men in seamen's short coats and stocking caps. They turned dark, unfriendly faces to Luke as he entered, looked him over with narrow-eyed interest, then turned back to their drinks.

A slender, neatly dressed man stood up behind the counter under the landing. He had a small pink rose in his lapel, a pencil thin mustache under a thin, pinched nose. His glance drifted superciliously over the Ranger's big slicker-clad frame.

"*Monsieur*—" he began.

"A room," Luke said briefly. "For several days."

The clerk nodded. "Upstairs, *monsieur.*" He flicked at the ends of his mustache, his black eyes sharp and observant on Luke's face. "I am Pierre, *monsieur.* You are wet, no? Too bad one cannot do much about the weather—it is a pity, no?"

Luke grinned, and the voluble hotel man lifted his shoulders in resigned rebellion. "*Sacré bleu!* What rain!" He turned the register book around to face Riatt. "But perhaps *monsieur* would like some brandy first—?"

"Later."

Pierre shrugged. "You have baggage?"

Luke's tone was dry, humorous. "Two dead men."

Pierre's eyes widened abruptly, and Luke added levelly: "Perhaps I should see the undertaker first. Or Constable Jenkins. He is the law in Lafitte, no?"

Pierre nodded mechanically. "*Monsieur* La-Fronte is the undertaker. He is also the pharmacist. You will find his place around the next corner—on Gulf Street. The constable's office is in the Lawson Building, farther up the avenue."

Luke placed a gold piece on the counter in front of the clerk. "I'll be back," he promised.

The hotel man straightened. "What name, *monsieur?* On the register?"

Luke's eyes held a bleak smile. "Just write me down as Available Smith." He turned and went out, leaving the Frenchman staring.

Pierre repeated the name, rolling it on his lips. Then his Gallic temper exploded. "A room he wanted! Two dead men for baggage!" He shook his small fist toward the door. "A jokaire for a guest! Have I not had enough trouble these past weeks—?"

Outside the rain was thinning; the brunt of the squall had passed over Lafitte.

The big dun snorted impatiently as Luke hit his wet saddle. "I don't like this weather either," the Ranger growled. "We'll hunt up a warm stall and get some feed into you as soon as I turn these two bodies over to the law."

The burdened Open A animals followed behind the dun as Luke headed up the street. They came almost immediately to the first corner Luke had encountered on Orleans Avenue.

A rider formed out of the darkness on the road, moving toward Luke at a fast trot. He cut in behind Luke and rode on for about twenty yards before an impression registered between his prominent ears. Then he jerked his cayuse to a sliding halt, swiveled in the saddle, and glanced back to the intersection where Luke and the trailing, burdened animals had vanished.

"Sure looked like Tully an' Slim," he muttered. He was a tall, raw-boned man in range clothes and a slicker—a man not given to reckless judgments. But the impression bothered him. He turned his horse and rode back to the intersection. He waited until he saw Luke turn in toward the Lawson Building. Then he reined about, kicked his cayuse's flanks and set it at a run down the short street that ended smack against the long tie-rail of the gambling house known as the Fortune Wheel.

Five horses huddled together at the rack. They all bore the Open A brand. A jangle of laughter and music spilled out into the night, riding the wind off the Gulf. The raw-boned rider left his animal with the others and hurried toward the door. . . .

CHAPTER THREE

— A Bad Habit —

Luke Riatt pulled up and dismounted before the Lawson Building, a flat-roofed, two-story brick structure on the edge of the business section. Only two windows on the ground floor were stained by dim lamplight. Across one was the painted information: "Office of the Town Constable."

Luke paused by the window, glanced inside. He saw no one. But an oil light, wick turned low, was on a wall bracket over a rolltop desk at the far end of the office.

The Ranger tried the door, found it unlocked and walked inside.

He immediately heard snoring—a rumbling, uneven sound as if the sleeper had asthma. Luke frowned, his glance moving across the unswept floor to the gun rack on the near wall, the "wanted" posters tacked carelessly on the boards beside it.

The snoring seemed to come from behind the desk. Luke walked to it, put his hands on the high top and looked over it—down on the biggest hunk of humanity he had seen in a long time!

Then he noticed, somewhat discomfited, that he was also looking down the muzzle of a long-barreled Army Colt!

Luke's wet face showed no expression. The huge man with the nickel-plated badge on his black vest stirred in his chair.

I thought you were asleep," Luke growled.

"Was," the big man grunted. He had a soft, sleepy voice. "Sleep like a cat—ten times a day, half-hour at a time." His smile was as trusting as a child's. But he didn't put up his gun. Small, baby blue eyes inventoried Riatt.

Then he heaved himself to his feet, shoving his swivel chair back to the wall. Luke measured the lawman across the desk. He was not more than five feet seven—and probably nudged the scales at three hundred pounds. The man looked as big around as he was tall, and the Ranger judged that little of this girth was fat. He had short arms that bulged massively above the elbows. Standing, his legs had the thick solidity of oak stumps.

"Bad night for travelin'," the lawman pointed out. His voice indicated no real interest in Luke's problems. But he added politely: "You in trouble?"

The Ranger eyed the Colt that lay like a squirt gun in the man's big hand. "None I can't handle myself," he said flatly. "But I ran into two hombres who couldn't handle theirs." He jerked a thumb over his shoulder. "They're outside. Dead. I brought them in."

The lawman had a round, olive-skinned face. Close-shaven, it resembled that of a fat, contented baby. Blue eyes enhanced that illusion.

He made a small, negative motion with his shoulders. "Why here?"

Temper crept into Riatt's tone. "Sign on your window says this is a law office. That badge on your vest tells me you're the law!"

"You always believe what you see?"

Small, dangerous flecks appeared in Luke's eyes. He nodded grimly. "Usually."

The big man came around his desk, making little noise. He walked to the front door like a crab, moving sidewise, one eye on Luke. He made a motion with his Colt.

Riatt walked to the door. The lawman glanced out into the night and eyed the three horses nudging the rail. His gaze held for a moment on the bodies draped across the saddles of the Open A horses.

Then he turned to face Luke. "Where?" His tone held only a mild interest.

"Ran into them about five miles west of town," Riatt answered. "The short feller took a .45 slug in his stomach. The thin one was killed by someone using a knife— or a sword."

The lawman considered this in his bland, unconcerned way. Impatience suddenly charged

45

the Ranger's voice. "Take it any way you want, Constable!" he said sharply. "They're not my trouble now—they're yours!"

He started for the door, but the Constable's Colt came up, centering on Luke's belt line.

"Just a minute," the man said. A dry chuckle crept into his voice. "I'm Gosh Jenkins. Who are you?"

Riatt paused less than a good arm's length from the constable. The warning specks multiplied in his eyes, but the ponderous law officer ignored them.

"Put that gun away, Jenkins," the Ranger said softly, "and I might tell you."

The constable's blue eyes widened and his chuckle turned harsh. "Now, sonny," he chided Luke coldly, "you wouldn't get tough, would you?"

Raitt's eyes held a wicked gleam. "Put that Colt away," he murmured, "or use it!"

The big lawman's face twisted in a sneer. "Why, you poor fool!" He took half a step forward, bringing his Colt up fast for a short, chopping blow at Luke's head.

He didn't see the big Ranger move. He felt iron fingers close around his thick, hairy wrist, checking his swing as though he had rammed his arm into a stone wall. Before he could shift the enormous power of his shoulders behind that arm, Luke's right Colt muzzle

46

jammed violently into his barrel stomach.

Jenkins grunted, his mouth springing open from the shock. Pain washed the bright color from his eyes. For a moment he was helpless, trying to suck in a breath. Riatt twisted the Colt from his fingers, stepped back and tossed it into a corner of the room.

"I'm as peaceful as the next man, Constable," he said grimly. "But I have a couple of bad habits. One of them is that I get nervous when a gun is pointed at me!"

Jenkins was gulping in air now, his arms hanging limp at his sides. His eyes were no longer baby blue. They were flat-hued, the color of scratched flint.

"I'll remember that," he said painfully. "But I'm still asking you, mister—who in the devil are you?"

Luke chuckled coldly. "I'm registered at the Pierre House as Available Smith."

Jenkins took a deep breath. The color started coming back into his coffee-hued face. He shuffled away from the open door and sank into a straight chair against the wall.

"Let's start at the beginning," he persisted grimly. "What happens outside of this town doesn't interest me. That's the county sheriff's job. He gets paid for it. I don't. But what happens in Lafitte is my business."

He took another breath, sucking his lips in

against his stubby teeth. "You tell me you pick up two dead men and bring them in to me. Why? A range bum would have been smart enough to let the bodies lay where he found them. You don't look like a range bum to me. And no drifter ever saw the day he could own a cayuse like you got tied up outside." His eyes narrowed angrily. "That's why it boils down to two choices for me. Either you're wearing a badge under your coat—or you're running from the law. I want to know which."

Riatt considered this reasonable request. Joseph Russell, the customs chief, had led him to expect a different man in Lafitte. The G. Jenkins who had written his reports of the Morse and Drake killings had sounded like a stiff and ineffectual lawman. The man who faced him was neither.

The Ranger could think of no good reason Jenkins shouldn't know who he was and why he had come to Lafitte. He had to start somewhere, Riatt reasoned, and Jenkins struck him as the kind of man who knew more than he had written to Joseph Russell.

Luke nodded. "We could have come to that sooner, if you had been more polite," he said. He slid his gun back into holster, brought his hands up to his coat pocket and handed his credentials to Jenkins, who glanced narrow-eyed at the Ranger badge.

"I'm Luke Riatt," Luke said briefly.

Jenkins' lips sucked in sharply. He nodded coldly. "I've heard of you," he said.

Luke shrugged. He slipped his credentials back into his pocket. "We'll let the name Available Smith ride for a while, Jenkins," he suggested.

Jenkins nodded. He got up and walked over to his desk and leaned against it, his manner suddenly respectful.

"I expected Mister Russell would send another man to Lafitte," he said. "But I didn't expect the Rangers——" his smile twisted bleakly—— "or the famed Luke Riatt!"

Riatt frowned. "I happened to be available," he said shortly. "Russell was short-handed."

The big constable's voice slipped back into its accustomed blandness. "I know your reputation, Luke," he said. "But I think Russell sent you down on a wild goose chase. I don't know what you expect to find——"

"Who killed Bert Morse and Carl Drake," Luke inserted bluntly, "and why. Joe Russell seemed to think that was important, Jenkins."

A faint sneer was mirrored in Jenkins' eyes. "I wrote him why his men were killed. A half-breed named Enrico with a skinful of liquor thought Morse was trying to beat his time with Lolita and used a knife on him. I don't know who killed Drake. Blazes, Luke—this is a port town. Some beef from the ranges up north are still trailed down here, sold and shipped on

49

hoof aboard side-wheelers for New Orleans and Florida markets. Then there's ships from half a dozen foreign ports put in here. The crews are tough—and they hang out at the Fortune Wheel when they come ashore." He shrugged. "The man who killed Carl Drake could have gone out on the next morning's tide."

Riatt said mildly, "Russell didn't see it that way, Jenkins."

"To the devil with Russell!"

Luke shrugged. "I didn't know Morse or Drake. I don't know what they ran into down here. But Joseph Russell knew them both. And he seemed sure of one thing. He was sure Carl Drake didn't get himself killed over an entertainer in the Fortune Wheel!"

Jenkins reached inside his shirt pocket for a long Mexican cheroot. He was silent while he struck a match and got the cheroot going.

"Mister Russell is in Austin, Luke," he finally said. "He sits behind a big desk a long way from Lafitte. Two of his men get killed, and he doesn't like it. Neither do I. But I was here! And I know where I found Carl Drake's body!"

"Where?"

Jenkins took the cigar out of his mouth and spat out shreds of tobacco. "In a place a dozen men would knife their way to reach! In Lolita's bedroom!"

Riatt shook his head. "Drake didn't come here

50

for that kind of fun. I think I'll go along with Russell on Carl. He was in Lafitte because Bert Morse stumbled onto something. Bert didn't have a chance to file a report with Russell's office, but he might have communicated with Drake. I understand they worked as a team in this area. Whatever it was, it had something to do with the Empress Carlotta's jewels—or what someone thinks are Carlotta's jewels." Luke frowned. "A town like this, pretty much isolated on the coast, would seem to be the kind of place smugglers would seek out."

Jenkins scowled. "If you say so. I got enough on my hands here without checking on jewel smugglers. As you say, this is a tough town. Up to a week ago I had two assistants. One is still in bed—he tried to break up a fight in a waterfront dive. The other quit. Said he had stomach trouble." He stood up, his lips clamped hard around his thin cigar. "I've been doing the work of three men and getting paid for one. I get paid for breaking up fights, discouraging thieves, keeping the tough joes in line. I don't get paid for checking on smugglers."

Riatt nodded coldly. "I get paid to check up on trouble, any kind of trouble," he said bluntly. "Down here it seems to be smuggling." He changed the subject abruptly, sensing the stubborn attitude of the constable. "Where can I find this entertainer, Lolita?"

51

"In the Fortune Wheel. The girls live upstairs, on the third floor. You passed it on your way here. The big gambling hall sitting back on the edge of the bluff."

Jenkins heaved himself away from the desk. "I still don't like it, Ranger!" he said angrily. "I wrote the customs office what I found out. I don't like being checked up on!"

He made an angry gesture, stalling Luke's cold reply. "I didn't know why Bert Morse and Carl Drake came to Lafitte. I didn't even know who they were until I checked through their clothing. But I know *why* they were killed—and I'll stick to it!"

Riatt shrugged. "I'll take a look around, anyway," he said. "I promised Russell I'd do that for him."

Jenkins clamped a lid on his sneer. "All right," he muttered. "Look around. I wish you luck."

"Thanks," Luke said dryly. He walked to the door, paused to glance at the horses shifting uncomfortably in the thin rain. Tully's body reminded him of the statuette in his saddle bag.

He turned. "One more thing, Jenkins," he said, keeping his voice casual. "You ever run across a clay cat, black, about so high, with green jade eyes and a kind of insolent grin under his whiskers?"

Jenkins' teeth bit down on his cheroot. "Cat?" He shook his head. "Cripes, Ranger—you must have had a hard day." He paused, frowning, listening to the clatter of horsemen coming up the avenue.

Riatt stepped out to the canopied boardwalk, eyeing the five riders looming up out of the night. They swung sharply in to the law office rack and pulled up behind the cayuses already there.

A raw-boned man in range garb peeled out of his saddle, his palm hitting the bone handle of his Colt. His voice cracked a sharp accusation.

"That's Tully an' Slim, Myles, like I said!" He palmed his Colt, his glance lifting to the big Ranger facing him on the walk. "An' there's the son who bushwhacked them!"

CHAPTER FOUR

— Too Many Corpses —

The big ranger stood flat-footed on the edge of the walk, a faint smile on his lips. Out of the corner of his eyes he saw Jenkins squeeze his big bulk through the door. The constable planted himself in front of the window, slightly behind and to the left of Riatt, hooking his right thumb in his belt above his empty holster.

"You looking for trouble, Myles?" he asked caustically. He wasn't looking at the man who had dismounted; he was eyeing the rider in the middle of the group.

Luke's gaze studied this man who was evidently in authority over the other riders: a blond man in his mid-thirties, slightly shorter than six feet, with a good pair of shoulders; a vain man who had not yet let vanity turn him soft. He was wearing an expensive gray suit, and a heavy gold watch chain made two loops across his vest. His left hand, resting on his pommel, was graced by a thick gold band topped by a red garnet around his ring finger.

He was frowning, evidently weighing Jenkins' question. His voice had overtones of puzzlement when he said: "You keep out of this, Jenkins!"

Luke's attention had swung back to the raw-boned man, who had evidently come primed for trouble. Jenkins' intrusion into the scene disconcerted him; he turned to look back at the Open A trail boss. The other three riders, range hands from their dress, sat slack in the saddle. They seemed to have come as spectators, Luke reflected coldly. And then he set himself for the trouble he saw coming.

Jenkins' voice held a warning rasp. "Rein in your foreman, Myles, or he'll get hurt!"

Myles Hegstrom shook his head. "You're a town cop, Myles. Stay that way!" He turned his cold gaze on Luke. "Mister, Tully and Slim worked for me. I thought they were back at the chuck wagon—but I see I was wrong. I want to know what happened to them."

Luke's voice reached out with bleak irony. "Then you're one step behind your gun-proddy foreman. *He* knows what happened—he thinks!"

The raw-boned ramrod jerked around. He was standing between Luke's big dun and ˙ Slim's buckskin, and he had the advantage of a gun in his hand. The dun was between him and Riatt, up on the walk, its bulk protecting him from Luke, and he saw no reason to stall his play.

Luke's voice rang out before he could lift his Colt across the dun's saddle: "Quarter, boy— quarter! "

The dun crowded the Open A man, jamming

him against the buckskin. The buckskin gave ground, but was stopped by Tully's gray mare. The big dun kept jamming the cursing ramrod against Slim's bronc.

Luke stepped out into the street just as the man wrenched free of the crowding animals. "Next time pick out cover that won't move," Luke suggested contemptuously.

The gunman whirled. He still had his Colt in his hand. He took two quick steps backward to get Riatt into clear view and jerked the muzzle upward. . . .

No one saw the gun until it appeared in Luke's fist. The muzzle blast laid its brief illumination over the wet cobbles, staining them an eerie red. . . .

The ramrod jerked. His Colt went off, but the muzzle was tilted skyward, and the brief glare showed the shock on his heavy-boned face. Luke's slug had shattered his elbow. He was still clinging to his gun, and he was surprised at this. The surprise lasted a brief moment; then pain hit him!

Jenkins' voice ripped harshly across the night. "Myles! I told you you were making a mistake! Smith didn't kill Tully and Slim. He ran across their bodies by French Creek and packed them into town, like any law-abiding citizen would."

Myles was staring at Luke, surprise lingering on his face. "Reckon Will Brenner was way ahead of himself," he apologized coldly. He leaned forward slightly, clasping his hands on his wet pommel. "Smith, did you say?"

Luke Riatt nodded curtly.

"Puncher?"

"Sometimes."

Myles Hegstrom turned his glance to Jenkins as the constable's chuckle reached him. "Friend of yours, Gosh?" he growled.

Jenkins made a neutral gesture with his hands. "Never saw him before tonight," he answered truthfully.

Myles Hegstrom seemed puzzled by this. He turned back to Luke, ignoring his ramrod, who was slowly backing toward his horse. Brenner's teeth were clenched against the pain that threatened to turn his stomach.

"I trail-bossed six hundred head of Open A beef to Lafitte, Smith," Myles explained bluntly. "Finished loading them into shipping pens yesterday. Tully and Slim worked for me. I admit we made a mistake jumping you like this. If you're looking for a job, you've got one right now." He looked down at his foreman, his glance impersonal. "Brenner's job!"

The wounded man stopped. His Colt still dangled from his nerveless fingers. He looked up at Myles, his face slack with pain. Then the full import of Hegstrom's callous dismissal got through to him.

57

His teeth unclenched enough to let a single bitter expletive through. He grabbed his dangling Colt with his left hand and tore it free. His thumb slipped off the bloody hammer as he swiveled it up to blast Hegstrom.

He didn't get a second chance.

The Open A boss dipped his right hand inside his coat. A snub-nosed .38 pistol hammered Brenner into abrupt silence. The foreman straightened as the bullet tore into him, looked up into the sky. Rain fell into his slackening face. Then his knees buckled and he fell heavily.

Hegstrom slipped his pistol out of sight. "The darn fool!" His voice was harsh, holding little regret.

Riatt walked slowly to his dun's side. He had the strange feeling that there was more to this than Will Brenner's too quick jump to a conclusion. Brenner had come gunning for him, but his reasons extended beyond the avenging of Slim and Tully.

Hegstrom made one last bid to Luke. "Will be needing a couple of hands. The job's wide open, Smith."

Riatt shook his head. He stepped up into the dun stallion's saddle and glanced at Jenkins. The constable had a strange smile on his round face. He raised his hand in a brief goodbye. "Drop by again, Smith."

Riatt shrugged. The rain came full into his face as he swung his horse away from the rack, avoided Brenner's body and headed back for the Pierre House.

Jenkins waited until the Ranger had faded into the rain-swept darkness. Then he turned his attention to the Open A boss. "You poor fool!" he bit out, shaking his head. "You swizzle-headed, danged fool!"

Hegstrom's thick neck bulged. "I don't have to take that from you, Gosh—" he began.

"You'll take it!" Jenkins snapped. His tone had a cut to it that stilled the backlash of Hegstrom's anger. "You've got three dead men on your hands! Even for Lafitte, that's too many corpses lying around. Get the mover to Lafronte's parlors. Now!"

Hegstrom choked back his reply. He turned to his men, his orders curt. "Get Brenner, Tully and Slim to the funeral parlors. I'll join you in a few minutes."

He waited until his men had turned the corner before riding up to the now empty tierack and dismounting. Jenkins was already inside his office, pacing the dirty floor.

The Open A man closed the door, shook water from his expensive pearl gray Stetson and ran his fingers through his hair. He tossed the hat angrily on the chair. "I'm not sorry about gunning Brenner!" he snapped. "The nosy buzzard was getting wind of things, anyway. But we could use a fast gun like Smith! Cripes! I didn't even see—"

"You triple-headed fool!" Jenkins snarled. "That was Luke Riatt who gunned Will Brenner! Texas Ranger!"

The anger went out of Hegstrom like air from a pricked balloon. He swept his hat off the chair and sat down. "I didn't figure on the Rangers when I agreed to this deal, Gosh," he muttered.

"Nobody did!" Jenkins lashed back. "But he's here. Walked in on me—said he had two dead men outside. What happened to Tully and Slim, anyway? How do they figure in this?"

Hegstrom licked his lips. "The darn fools walked into the Curio Shoppe this afternoon and bought the cat!"

"What?"

"I didn't know about it!" Hegstrom growled back defensively. "They got through chousing steers into the pens yesterday and said they had never been in a seaport town before. Wanted to see the sights. I let them go. Tonight I ride in to pick up the cat." He made an empty gesture with his hands.

Jenkins' tone was incredulous. "Therese turned it over to them?"

"No. The old girl was out when they walked in. Her stepdaughter, Justine, was in the shop

60

alone. She sold them the cat for five dollars!"

Hegstrom stood up and stooped to pick up his hat. "I rode over to the Fortune Wheel to join some of my boys. My job is to pick up the cat. That's my end of this deal, Gosh!"

Jenkins was looking toward the windows, not listening.

Hegstrom shrugged angrily. "I sent Brenner back to camp to see if Tully and Slim had checked in. Will rode back a few minutes ago and ran across Luke Riatt heading for your place. I was waiting at the bar when he came in with the news. Dang it, Gosh!" he burst out. "Listen to me!"

Jenkins turned, a thin smile on his lips.

"I didn't know what to make of it!" Hegstrom snarled. "But Brenner was in a mean mood after riding back from camp, and I egged him into gunning for the man who had brought Slim and Tully here. If Slim and Tully had bought the cat, then it was still in their possession—or this hombre who was bringing their bodies in had it. It would have worked out fine —if it had been anyone but this Ranger Riatt."

Jenkins grunted. He walked across the room and picked up his Colt. He held it thoughtfully in his big hand, remembering the man who had taken it from him as easily as though he had been a child. The memory gnawed at him.

There were faster men with a Colt—this he

conceded. But he had never met a man he couldn't manhandle. He dropped his Colt into his holster and raised his hands to look at them.

Hegstrom's voice was petulant. "There's going to be the devil to pay when Jules finds out!"

"I think he's already found out!" Jenkins said. "Slim was killed with a sword!"

The Open A boss winced. He jammed his hat on his head. "I've had enough, Gosh. Cat or no cat, I'm pulling out in the morning!"

"You'll stay!"

Hegstrom met the constable's glance, recognizing the temper in the big man's sleepy gaze. "I'll stay until the weekend," he compromised sullenly. He walked to the door, yanked it open and stamped out.

Jenkins watched him wheel his horse away from the tierack and head into the night at a gallop. He walked out, stopping by the post supporting the wooden awning. A fine rain sifted into his face. The avenue was empty as far as he could see.

He had known that inevitably the law would close in on Lafitte. The two customs men had been the first. He had expected others to follow. But not Luke Riatt!

The challenge stirred his blood, bringing a glitter of anticipation to his eyes. In a way, he was glad it was the big Ranger who had come. It gave him a perverse pleasure, roused in him a

CHAPTER FIVE

— The Death of Wichita Jones —

Luke Riatt rode back to The Pierre House and turned his dun down the alley leading to the stables on the narrow back street a block away. The stallion splashed in the puddles that were fetlock deep in front of the barn. A faint yellow light came through the small opening in the big door.

The Ranger dismounted and shoved the heavy door back on its runners. The sour smell of the enclosure wafted out to him, crinkling his nose.

A thin, querulous voice came from the shadows at the far end of the barn. "Yassum boss. Jest a minnit."

Riatt waited. A stooped, lanky Negro came shuffling into the light of the lantern hanging from a nail on the wall. Straw clung to his baggy pants. There was even straw in his hair, which sprouted like a puff of gray cotton on his head.

The hostler's eyes rolled as he saw the big gleaming-hided stallion behind Riatt. "Ain' seed a animal like him since I left Kaintucky, boss." He ran his palm along the dun's flank and the stallion turned his head and eyed him. "It's all right, big boy," the Negro said. He liked

primitive need to test his strength against this man whose prowess was becoming legend.

His big hand closed around the post, a gust of emotion shaking him. . . .

"Save your strength, Gosh," a voice suggested calmly.

Jenkins turned. A small, wiry figure came out of the shadows across the street. A black cape fluttered from the man's narrow shoulders. He came up to the walk with a quick light stride, brushed past Jenkins and went inside the law office.

Jenkins shuffled in after him, kicking the door shut. "Some day you'll catfoot it up to a man who'll shoot first, Jules," he muttered grimly

"He'll have to see me," the other said dryly. He was an old man, and the years had drawn their fine lines on the parchment of his face. He carried a cane. But though he leaned on it often when in the public gaze, he had no real need of it. His body had been molded on the drill fields of France and tempered on its battlefields, and he still walked with a soldier's military erectness.

His eyes were small, black, vividly alive as they studied Jenkins. They were like the bright eyes of a small, quarrelsome bird. He even cocked his head to one side like a bird when he listened.

"I saw him leave," he said. Age had weakened

his voice, but not the authority implicit in it. "The big man—who is he?"

"Riatt," Jenkins answered sourly.

The old man frowned. "He must be disposed of. Quickly, but quietly."

Jenkins sighed. "Reckon you didn't get the name right off, Jules. That was Luke Riatt! Texas Ranger!"

Jules LeCoste allowed a small smile to break the thin line of his lips. "I have heard of him." He was not impressed. "I have heard of many men with reputations. They all die." He tapped the silver head of his cane lightly, a cynical light in his eyes. "Big or small, Jenkins—they all die!"

Jenkins nodded. "*He* won't be easy!"

The other shrugged. "Things have gone wrong," he conceded. "Hegstrom was to have picked up the cat today. Instead, two drunken fools walked in—" He walked to the chair and sat down. "Luckily I stopped by the shop shortly after they left. Therese told me what had happened."

He tapped his cane on the floor. Jenkins said wryly, his eyes on the walking stick, "I understand that you caught up with them."

Jules frowned. "I searched the tall one's saddlebags, but he didn't have the cat. The rain stopped me before I could follow the other one—the one called Tully."

"Riatt has the cat," Jenkins said. He walked to

the window and looked out into the dismal night. "I don't think he knows what it is worth or what's in it. He started to ask me about it just before Hegstrom and his boys showed up."

"I already assumed he had the cat." The old man nodded. "But perhaps, if he doesn't yet know its real value, he might be careless." He sighed and got to his feet. "We must make sure he doesn't find out, Jenkins."

The constable brought up his huge hands and clenched them. "I'll take care of Luke Riatt," he promised. "You take care of the cat—and Hegstrom!"

Jules looked at him. "Myles is not backing out?"

"He wanted to head back tomorrow," Jenkins said. "He's afraid of the Ranger."

The old man's lips crinkled. "He'll stay. I'll get the cat back tonight. And he'll pay us *before* he leaves this time. Fifty thousand dollars!"

Jenkins nodded. "You get the cat," he said harshly. "I'll take care of Luke Riatt!"

horses, and that liking was in his voice—he patted the stallion's strong neck. "This weather ain't good for a hoss like you, boy. I'll rub you down real gentle."

The dun's nostrils quivered, and his breath fluttered through them. Riatt smiled. "He doesn't general take to strangers," he said. "But he doesn't draw a color line when he does. I think you'll get along just fine."

"Wichita Jones, boss. I was born an' raised on a hoss farm." The hostler's teeth gleamed white against his black face. "I'll take good care of him, boss."

Riatt dropped a silver dollar into the man's palm. "I'll be around to see him in the morning, Wichita."

He paused in the door opening, war bag in hand. The stars made a pattern through rifts in the overcast. The wind was still blowing off the sea, laying its chill on the night. Rain had managed to get through the protection of his slicker, soaking the back of his neck and the top of his shoulders. He felt that wetness now, cold and unpleasant—but long years of living out in the open had inured him to the weather.

He stepped outside, skirted the big puddle in front of the barn door and headed up the alley. The affair at the law office still puzzled him. Will Brenner had come gunning for him with the open consent of his boss, Myles Hegstrom.

Why? The excuse that they thought he had killed Tully and Slim didn't hold water.

Nor had Gosh Jenkins helped matters. He had warned the Open A boss that Brenner would get hurt. But he could have stopped the shooting if he had told Myles flatly that Riatt had had nothing to do with the killing of the two Open A riders.

The big Ranger paused in front of The Pierre House. The rain had stopped. The wind ran clean and fresh through the wet streets of Lafitte. It was past midnight, but some part of the port town remained awake. The sounds of rough voices, the sudden jangle of breaking glass rode the reckless wind.

It took a strong man and a brave man to keep order in a town like this, Luke reflected. In a way the law problem in Lafitte paralleled that of the trail towns up north. The difference was that instead of contending with lonely, half wild punchers in town after two or three months on the trail, Lafitte was periodically invaded by restless, town-hungry men from the sea.

A big job for one man—but now that he had seen G. Jenkins, the Ranger revised his estimate of the constable. Jenkins' story had sounded plausible. And he had insisted that Bert Morse and Carl Drake had been killed over a woman —an entertainer in the Fortune Wheel.

Luke frowned. Maybe Jenkins was right—and

Joseph Russell wrong. But he had promised the customs chief he'd check. There was Drake's wife in Galveston, with two young children, and she did not believe Jenkins' report. Moreover, she deserved to know the truth!

Luke turned into the hotel. The bar was closed. An oil lamp on the desk clerk's counter cast a dim light in the narrow bar and lobby. An old man with a drooping mustache dozed behind the counter. He lifted his head as Luke rapped on the wood, brushed sleep from his eyes.

"I'm Smith," Luke said. "I checked in about two hours ago."

The night clerk ran his finger down the register, and Luke's glance, following, saw that another man had registered after him. Remington Drake!

The name jogged him. Drake was not an unusual name, and this man might not even know Carl Drake. But the possibility nagged at him. He checked the room number beside the new guest's name. 316. Luke's was 214.

It might be worth looking into, Luke thought grimly. He picked up his bag, took the key the old night clerk handed him and walked up the stairs. A lamp in a wall bracket guided him down the worn carpeting of the corridor. He walked until he saw the number 214 painted on a door, then inserted his key.

He pushed the door open. The room was dark and had the musty smell of closeness. He lighted a wooden match on his thumb nail, and his glance picked out the china-based lamp on the dresser by the bed. The match went out as he reached the lamp. He struck another, tilted the glass chimney, and the match flame fed across the trimmed wick.

He dropped his war bag by the bed and was getting out of his slicker when a voice said: "You look bigger against that light! Too big for me to miss!"

The Ranger turned around, one arm free of his slicker. Rain dripped from the folds and made a small dark puddle near his feet.

The man behind the door kicked it shut. Luke recognized him as the young fellow who had blocked him off on Orleans Avenue earlier. He had changed into dry clothes—a white shirt with the cuffs folded back and a pair of neat gray pants. The gun in his fist was the same one he had pulled on Riatt before.

His jaw was puffed out on the left side of his face, as though he had a bad toothache. It gave him a lopsided grin when he smiled. But his eyes were bright and unafraid when he looked at the Ranger.

"You're a sucker for punishment, son," Riatt murmured. "I'll say that much for you."

"I'm a gambler," the other corrected. "I learned

my lesson, big feller. You're tough and you're fast! All right; I'll play it this time with a stacked deck." He patted the muzzle of his Colt with his left hand. "I don't think you're fast enough to beat the odds in this joker, or tough enough to argue with a .45 slug!"

Riatt shrugged. "I still don't know why you picked me out for all this attention," he growled. "Who are you?"

The youngster made a grimace as he came away from the wall. "I'll ask the questions—and do the ordering!" His swollen jaw hindered his speech. "You shuck that gun belt; then we'll talk."

Riatt measured the youngster. He was old enough to be taken for a man in any company, yet young enough to be reckless—and he was not easily discouraged. But he wasn't the type to shoot a man without reason. The Ranger took this into consideration as he unbuckled his gun belt and let it fall at his feet. Then he kicked it out of the way and finished shedding his slicker.

With Luke's gun out of reach the youngster relaxed a little. Luke had the slicker in his hands. He turned as if to drop it on the bed—and dropped it over the lamp instead!

Then he whipped around and was halfway to Drake before darkness smothered all detail in the room.

Drake cursed. But he didn't shoot. He didn't

see anything to shoot at—and while he was cursing a rock-hard fist slammed him in the stomach, doubling him like an oiled hinge. He fell against Riatt, dropped his Colt and clawed at Luke's frame for support. A stubborn will dredged up some reserve of strength, shook off the numbing effects of Luke's blow. Still in close, he lashed out with a savage flurry of blows that surprised the Ranger.

Riatt finally caught the youngster's flailing arms and spun him around. His assailant was like sprung steel in his hands, twisting and slipping. In the dark, Luke missed him twice before he connected with a short, jolting uppercut to young Remington Drake's jaw.

He eased the suddenly limp figure to the floor, turned, and made his way back to the dresser. The faint unpleasant smell of hot rubber guided him. He eased the slicker off the lamp, scraped a match and lighted up.

Drake was pulling himself to his hands and knees when Riatt turned. Luke took two long strides to the youngster's Colt, tossed it on the bed. He did the same with his gun belt which was lying on the floor.

Luke's upper lip had been split by one of the youngster's blows and his ribs ached. Riatt ran his tongue over his cut and grinned sourly. Whoever this kid was, he was quite a scrapper for his size.

He walked over to Drake, hauled him to his feet and dropped him into a chair. The youngster started to get up, his eyes blazing. Luke put his palm against the man's shirt and shoved him back.

"All right, son," Luke said coldly. "You proved you're tough. Now tell me what you're after."

Drake's bloodied lips pulled tight against his teeth. "I'm after the man who killed my brother," he said harshly. "I'm Remington Drake."

Riatt straightened in surprise. "You're Carl Drake's brother?"

Remington nodded. He had his hands on the chair sides, and he seemed ready to spring up at Luke. "You knew my brother?" he asked bitterly.

Luke shrugged. "Only what Joseph Russell, head of the State Customs Department, told me. I'm Luke Riatt, Texas Ranger."

The tenseness left young Drake. He eased back against the horsehair padding and ran his tongue over his swelling lips. "Luke Riatt! No wonder I didn't get anywhere tangling with you!"

Riatt frowned. "I've had trouble with bigger men, and been hurt less," he growled.

Drake got to his feet. "I guess I acted like a young fool, Luke." His voice held a trace of chagrin. "I came to Lafitte on a black horse and with a mental picture of myself as Sir Galahad out to right a wrong." He smiled ruefully. "In

73

less than three hours I've had that notion beaten out of me." He eyed the big Ranger. "Sir Galahad is going to need help in this town, Luke."

Luke was not one for fancy allegory. "You *have* been leading with your chin," he said bluntly.

Young Drake touched his tender jaw. "Goes to show you what happens when a fellow steps out of character. I've been making my living for five years with a deck of cards. It's a profession taken up by cynics, not eighteenth century sentimentalists. But hang it, Luke, my brother wasn't that kind of man! He was the oldest of four boys, and the steadiest. He knew what he wanted early in his life. He wanted Ann, the girl he married, and he wanted kids. He took his job with the Customs Department seriously. That's why no two-bit lawman named G. Jenkins can convince me my brother started chasing some two-bit entertainer and got himself killed over her!"

Riatt shrugged. "How did you find out about Jenkins' report?"

"He mailed a copy to my sister-in-law," Drake snapped. "She enclosed it in a letter to me."

The Ranger ran his fingers through his damp hair. "Joe Russell, Carl's boss, didn't believe that about your brother, either. That's why I'm in town. But Gosh Jenkins sticks to his story. I had a talk with him tonight. And I've got a hunch he's going to be in our way when we start checking on it."

Drake let out a sharp breath. "To the devil with that two-bit town constable!"

"He's not that easy to brush aside." Luke grinned. "And I wouldn't advise you to get in his way. Not unless you like tangling with a grizzly!"

Rem Drake frowned. "I guess you know Carl was in Lafitte to track down jewel smugglers, Luke."

Riatt was peeling off his wet coat. He hung it on a bed post and looked at Drake. He nodded. "Russell seemed to think so. He got one report from your brother. Carl asked him for a description of the late Empress Carlotta's jewels."

Drake said grimly: "Then maybe you should read the letter I received from Carl. I'll get it. It's in my room, upstairs."

Luke walked to the lone window as Drake went out. Wooden shutters were closed against the squall that had lashed Lafitte. A couple of loose slats vibrated in the wind.

Luke opened the casement-type windows. They swung inward. A chill breeze came into the room, strong enough to flutter the leaves of a calendar on the far wall.

Drake came back then, holding a letter in his hand. He must have run up and down the stairs,

Luke thought, and he had a moment's wonder at the youngster's unbounded energy.

Rem Drake came up to him, holding out the letter. "I checked the cancellation date on it, Luke. Carl mailed this the day he was killed!"

Luke slipped the notepaper from the damp envelope and walked closer to the lamp. The ink had smudged a little, but the words were still legible:

Dear Rem:

You used to say you'd know when you were going to die. Remember? Well, kid, I've got that feeling today. I can't shake it. That's why I've decided to write this to you.

Bert Morse was killed here last week. I don't think you met Bert. He and I worked this area together. Bert kind of reminded me of you. Young, and too cocky for his own good sometimes. Restless as a she bear away from her cubs. Well, we had some business in Lafitte. But I wanted to drop by and see Ann and the boys. I hadn't been home in over a month. Bert said he'd meet me in town.

I got a note from him the day I was leaving to join him. It didn't make sense, especially if you know Bert. He took life as one big joke. There was wine, there were women, and there was trouble. That's the way he saw things—and to him they always added up to fun. But to get back to Bert's note—I didn't tell Ann about it—I didn't want to worry her. Bert wrote: "Ran into a redheaded lead. What do you know about the Empress Carlotta's jewels? Am waiting to pick up a black cat in the Curio Shoppe. Come quick. Need your fatherly advice. Best to Ann and the kids."

Bert was dead when I got here. Jenkins, the town constable, said Bert got into a fight with a half-breed name of Enrico over a girl; an entertainer in the Fortune Wheel, a local gambling house.

I checked on this entertainer, Lolita. She couldn't have been the redheaded lead Bert mentioned—she's a brunette.

Cripes, I'm getting writer's cramp, Rem, so I'll cut this letter short. There's a girl who works in the Curio Shoppe—a pretty, black-haired lass named Justine. I think she knows something about the smuggling Bert got wind of. I think the Curio Shoppe has a part in it.

If something happens to me, Rem, take

care of Ann and the boys. And if you come nosing around Lafitte, look out for a black cat; a statue about a foot high, with green jade eyes and the darnedest grin you ever saw. That's how Bert described it, and he seemed to think it was important.

Your brother,
Carl.

Riatt was frowning as he slid the letter back into its envelope. Drake said bitterly: "I walked right into it tonight. Ran smack into this girl Carl mentioned, Justine. I think she was running away from home." He recounted his meeting with her without elaboration.

"When I came to, she was gone. I hammered on the door of Madame Couet's, and finally someone stuck her head out of a window. I asked her if Justine had gone inside. She just closed the shutters and slammed the window down. I still had a headache when I rode out to the main street and ran into you." He rubbed his jaw ruefully. "Thanks for dragging me in out of the rain, Luke."

"How'd you know this was my room?"

Drake shrugged. "Felt pretty low when I finally dragged myself back into the saddle. So when I spotted this place I walked in. A crazy

78

Frenchman was behind the desk downstairs. He took one look at my jaw, at my muddy clothes, and started swearing in French. Then he asked me if I was available—and if my name, too, was Smith. Did I have baggage? How many dead men did *I* have with me?"

The Ranger was grinning.

"So when I finally got him calmed down," Drake continued, "he told me about the big man who had just left. From his description I knew he meant you. When I signed the register I noticed you were in room 214. So I washed, changed clothes and came down here to wait for you. The door was locked, but a skeleton key let me in. I'm glad I came, now."

Luke rubbed his knuckles across the stubble on his chin. "That black cat mentioned in your brother's letter—I've got it right here." He turned to the bed, then stopped. "No, I remember I left it in my saddle bag!"

He picked up Drake's colt and tossed it to the surprised youngster. He grabbed his own Colt, thrust it inside his belt. "Come on," he growled.

Remington Drake followed Luke out the door. They went down the dimly lighted stairs and out into the street. The cobbles of Orleans Avenue gleamed in the star shine.

A horse's angry whistling reached Riatt as he turned down the stable alley. In the still night the sound of shod hoofs splintering wood carried plainly.

The Ranger broke into a sprint. He splashed through puddles, skidded, banged up against the barn door. The opening was too narrow to let him inside. He jammed his shoulder against it, ran it back a couple of feet and twisted inside, his Colt ready in his hand.

The lantern was still burning in its place on the wall. Luke saw the dun's head rear high over the third stall down. The big stallion's eyes were rolling, his ears flattened back. He was lunging against the short length of rope holding him in the stall.

Luke ran down the straw-littered floor. Behind him he heard Drake splashing through the puddle in front of the barn.

Wichita Jones was sitting on the floor, his back resting against a big post. Pieces of the dun's stall boards lay around him. He had his head on his chest as if he were sound asleep.

Luke left him to Drake, pounding up behind him. The dun was shaking the entire building with his frantic lunging. Powerful hind legs kept splintering the barrier boards of his stall.

The stall to the left of the wild stallion was empty. Luke ducked into it and hauled himself up on the stall side. The dun turned to lunge at him, teeth bared, and Riatt caught a glimpse of what had set the animal off.

A long gash across his left hind quarter oozed blood!

"Easy, boy! It's me—Luke. Easy, boy!" He slid down into the stall with the pain-crazed stud, caught the dun's hackamore and held him quiet. Luke's voice was firm, soothing. "Easy, easy, boy!"

The stallion quieted down, his muscles quivering. Luke patted him reassuringly. "I'll get that cut fixed up," he promised. He came along the dun's flank, examined the long gash, his jaw tightening. "Hurt you, didn't he? Likes to use a knife, or a sword! He must have come in here looking for that black cat—"

He turned as Drake called out to him. "Better come over, Luke. I think he's trying to say something."

Riatt stepped over the remnants of the stall barrier and knelt beside Wichita Jones. That close, he could see the dark stain spreading over the hostler's ragtag shirt. He had the feeling that a closer examination would show that Wichita Jones had been run through the same way Slim had.

The Negro's eyes rolled. "Heard somebody movin', boss—heard the big boy—yore hoss-whistle. I came to see why. I—" He suddenly arched, his eyes rolling backward into his head. "I—" His breath gusted out.

Riatt waited a moment longer. But Wichita was dead. Luke got slowly to his feet. His saddle

81

was on the floor behind the post. His saddle bags had been ripped open. He knew the black cat was gone, but he searched through them anyway.

Drake asked slowly: "He got what he came after?"

Luke nodded. His jaw was like a chunk of granite as he faced the youngster. "It leaves us where we started, where Bert Morse and your brother started: at the beginning. But I know one thing now. Those two Open A drovers I brought into Lafitte weren't killed because of a woman. Nor was Wichita Jones. They were killed because of a black cat with jade eyes— and by the same man!"

Drake said stiffly: "My brother was stabbed to death, Jenkins wrote. So was Bert Morse."

Luke nodded grimly. "No matter what Constable Jenkins says, there's a connection." He glanced toward the door where a couple of men, pants pulled hurriedly up over long johns, were edging in.

He lowered his voice. "There's not much we can do tonight, Rem. But tomorrow we'll start where Bert started—at the Curio Shoppe. I've got a hunch that trail is going to lead us to the Fortune Wheel—and to a girl named Lolita!"

CHAPTER SIX

— Girl In The Attic —

The wind prowled under the eaves of Therese's house, and the mist off the sea filmed the small square lights of the lone window. The bells from the schooner, *Port of Call*, rolling at anchor in the cove, drifted into the room, ringing faintly in the ears of the sleepless girl.

She lay on the bed, staring up at the sloping ceiling. The bedside lamp, turned low, cast shadows in a slow, macabre dance on the peeling whitewash.

This had been home for seven years. This room had seen the transition from a gangling, dreamy-eyed girl to a young woman. It had memories inextricably bound with her future. But it was no longer home.

It was a small, dingy trap, and her destiny was in the hands of a small, leathery-skinned man she had once called "Uncle."

She lay still, fear scalding her throat. The wind prowled through the red slate roof shingles, moaning and sighing. She had loved this room, and its nearness to the stars, and the view she had of the cove from the window.

She stirred now, her attention caught by the

slamming of a door somewhere within the house. She got up from the bed, staring at the closed door. She had it bolted from her side. Outside in the hallway, Etienne stood guard like some great St. Bernard. He slept quietly, his breathing soft and deep and barely heard above the wind.

Justine turned to the window. The schooner lay against the dark water, its mast lights bobbing slowly. There was little at night to indicate where the bluffs ended and the dark sea began.

She wondered what had happened to the young man who had tried to help her.

She turned quickly now as someone came to the door. She heard Etienne move, but he uttered no sound. She faced the door, waiting. The knock was quiet, almost hesitant.

Justine said: "Yes?"

Her stepmother's voice reached her through the panels. "Open, Justine. I wish to have a few words with you."

Justine said nothing. Her eyes turned bitter.

"Quickly, before Monsieur LeCoste comes back." As Justine hung back, Therese said impatiently: "Would you rather I had Etienne break down the door?"

Justine crossed slowly and unbolted the door. Therese stood in the hallway, a small lamp in her hands. Behind her loomed Etienne. She came inside Justine's room, closed the door, and placed the lamp on a small chest near the wall.

She turned and eyed Justine closely, noting her red eyes.

"It is well, those tears," she said brusquely. "Because of your foolishness a fortune was nearly lost."

"A fortune that did not belong to you, or to *Monsieur* LeCoste," the girl said. "A fortune which you were unwilling to reveal, even to me."

Therese shrugged. "We all talk too much," she said coldly. "The fewer who knew, the less likely there would be a slip." She crossed to Justine, took her by the arm. "But I did not come to berate you again for having sold the cat to the wrong man. No, I came because—"

She paused, her shiny black eyes searching Justine's drawn face. "You are not my daughter," she said finally. "But I have always treated you well, no?"

Justine nodded slowly, her voice choked. "And I have worked for you and for *Monsieur* LeCoste as a daughter should."

Therese shrugged. "As a daughter, yes. But you were never that, you understand." As Justine stared at her: "I told you I married your father in Mexico, that he was a member of Maximilian's guard. You were his daughter, yes, but not mine. Your mother had died when you were a baby. She was a lady-in-waiting to the Empress Carlotta, as I was."

Justine looked at her. "Why are you telling me this now, Therese?"

"Because I do not want you killed!" Therese said coldly. "And so you will understand why I will not interfere with Jules if you do not do as he says—not even to save your life!"

Justine turned back to the window. Her gaze sought out the dark sand spit and the small block building on it. She shivered. "You want me to go there with him?"

"Only until things have quieted down here in Lafitte—until the last payment is made. Then we will take the first boat to Vera Cruz, and from there the great cities of the world are ours to choose."

Justine turned to her, her lips quivering. "Two men have died, Therese. How many more must die before we sail for Vera Cruz?"

"As many as will get in our way!" Therese said harshly. "All these years of planning—do you think we will throw them away now?"

Justine shook her head. She turned slowly to the small crucifix hanging on the wall by the bed; her voice was low. "You brought me up as yours. You taught me my prayers; you told me, at your knee, that there was right and there was wrong. And every Sunday you took me to Mass."

"We are only human," Therese said coldly. "We live our lives between the devil and the angels!"

86

She turned and picked up her lamp. "At dawn you will go with Etienne. He will take you to the island. You will stay there until we are ready to sail."

She walked to the door, looked back at Justine. Her face softened. "You are young, and the world is big—bigger than Lafitte. Perhaps, some day, we will even go back to Paris."

"Wherever we go," Justine said bitterly, "they will follow us, the dead men."

Therese shook her head. "The dead follow no one, *ma fille*. They remain dead."

She opened the door and went out, closing it behind her, closing it on the dark, impassive face of Etienne.

Justine turned and hurried to the door and bolted it; she backed away from it slowly, tears starting down her face. Out of the night came the sound of six bells, chiming softly, carried to her from the schooner riding out the tail of the squall in the cove. . . .

The banging of a loose shutter awakened Luke Riatt. He rolled over and sat up, blinking sleepily at the casement window. He ran his fingers through his crisp black hair, memory coming back to him, bringing a frown to his hard-angled face. The shutter banged shut again, and he got up and walked to the window. A strong wind was shoving against the slats.

Luke pushed the shutter open, leaned out and hooked the iron catch in place. He did the same to the other.

The wind blew in hard against him, and he felt the taste of the sea again, unfamiliar but somehow pleasant, sharp and tangy in his nose.

He looked across the flat roofs to the white-caps speckling the gray cove waters. The *Port of Call* lay off shore, sails furled tight. It rode steady against the strong wind, its anchor line taut against the drag of the sea.

The Ranger's glance held on that wooden ship; then he let his eyes follow the restless swell of the sea to the distant horizon. The wind that came from some distant point beyond his vision had a high, lonely sound that Luke Riatt recognized.

For Luke was part of that loneliness. For him there was always the far horizon, the trail beyond the distant butte, the road across the river. Some years ago he had made his choice; it was the way he wanted it.

But for the moment his mood was as gray and dismal as the sea, and he listened to the cry of the wind, not thinking thoughts but letting the past cast up its mental images of bygone events.

Then his attention was caught by the skiff that inched into view from some point of shore hidden from him. The early morning grayness blurred detail, but Luke made out the figure of a girl huddled in the stern of the small boat. A big man, a Negro, strained at the oars.

The skiff seemed to crawl against the wind, fighting the chop of the cove. Luke watched it skirt the schooner lying at anchor, disappear behind it. He judged they were headed for the narrow island that protected the cove from the heavier seas of the open Gulf.

Riatt turned from his window at the knock on his door. "Come in," he said.

Remington Drake stepped inside and closed the door. He had added a black string tie and a coat to the clothes he had worn the previous night, and Luke saw that he had shaved, though it must have hurt to run a razor over the bruises on his jaw.

"Ever lock your door?" Drake asked pleasantly.

"Sometimes."

"You might have had a visitor," the youngster said. He was grinning. "A gent who likes to work nights—with a sword!"

"I was hoping he would show up," Luke answered bleakly. He walked to the bed, sat down and pulled on his boots. "You're up mighty early," he observed. "I thought gamblers stayed up late and slept all morning."

Young Drake hooked a toe under a chair rung, dragged it to him and sat straddling it, facing Luke, his arms folded across the top. "Only when they work," he answered Luke cheerfully.

"You on vacation?"

"Call it that, Luke," Drake nodded. But the cheerfulness went out of his eyes and he changed the subject abruptly. "You hungry?"

Luke reached for his coat. He stood tall and broad-chested and as lean-flanked as a desert wolf. "Hungry enough to buy your breakfast and eat it, too," he growled. He buckled his cartridge belt on under his coat, and they went downstairs together. An old, straggly-haired woman was mopping up around the bar; she gave them a bleary smile.

The wind hit them as they stepped outside. It had a rawness that brought a shiver to young Drake. "Coffee's gonna taste good this morning," he muttered. "Hey! Where're you headed?"

"I want to look at my horse," Luke snapped.

They went down the muddy alley to the stables. The door was closed and barred from the inside. Luke frowned. He went around to the far side and found a small door that was unlocked.

The lantern had gone out during the night, but daylight, seeping in through a dirty window, provided some visibility. Luke walked surefooted through the poor light, Drake at his heels. The big dun had been put in a new stall. He turned his head and whinnied his recognition as Luke stepped inside with him.

The stallion muzzled Luke against the stall side, tongue licking over him, knocking Luke's hat from his head.

"Easy, you darn fool," Luke said. But his voice was gentle with affection. This big animal was the only real friend he had, the only companion he could count on.

He examined the slash the veterinarian (roused from his bed in the early hours of the morning) had treated. He saw no sign of inflammation. "Looks all right," he murmured. "Hind quarter will be stiff for a few days, but you'll be all right."

He shoved the muzzle away. "You're lucky. Nothing to do for the next few days except eat all the feed you can hold. Probably get fat on me."

The dun cut him off with a shove. Luke grinned.

He stepped out and dropped the stall bars in place, and Drake said grudgingly: "Wish I had a horse like that."

The big Ranger didn't comment. He was looking down at the post where Wichita Jones had died; died because he liked horses and had come to see what was troubling the big dun.

He'd had the cat in his saddle bag, and now it was gone. And he was right back where Bert and Carl Drake had started, where he would have to start—at the Curio Shoppe.

He turned to Drake, his smile grim. "Come on; we've got some shopping to do. We're looking for a black cat about eighteen inches high, and with the sassiest grin you ever saw. . . ."

CHAPTER SEVEN

—The Cat Maker —

The Curio Shoppe was stained with last night's rain, its windows shuttered. The door was locked. There was no sign to indicate whether the closing was due only to the early morning hour or was permanent. Wide roller shades hid the shop window's display and prevented a glimpse into the interior. It threw back their reflection, bleak against the gray morning sky.

Riatt turned to Drake. "Let's have that breakfast. We can try again—later."

They kept in close to the building line. The Sea Urchin's sign, creaking in the wind, caught their attention, and they went inside. Luke glanced casually at the group of seamen seated around two rear tables. They had a clanny affinity that marked them as members of the same ship's crew—quite possibly the schooner, *Port of Call*, lying at anchor in the cove. One of them, a burly, bearded fellow, eyed Luke pugnaciously, turning to sneer some remark into the ear of his companion.

Two other customers, townsmen by their dress, occupied widely separated stools at the long counter. They were minding their own business with poker-faced seriousness, obviously not wishing to get involved with the brawl-seeking sailors.

Luke and young Drake ordered ham and eggs and coffee. The service was fast, and the counterman, a thin, balding man occupied with his own personal troubles, did not bother them with garrulous gossip.

The sailors were resting up after an all night binge. They had recovered enough to feel mean, and they were obviously looking for trouble. The burly man kept referring to "cow nurses" and "dudes." Finally he took a more direct approach.

Luke was reaching in his pocket for money to pay for the breakfasts when the sailor jostled him.

The Ranger turned around on his stool. The burly man stood over him, his hands balled inside the pockets of his pea coat. "Why don't you keep your elbows where they belong, cow nurse!" he growled pugnaciously.

Luke looked him over with a thoughtful frown. "Maybe I ought to jam them into your ugly face," he suggested mildly.

The burly seaman yanked his hands out of his pockets and drove his right fist for Luke's face!

The Ranger ducked into the man, his hard shoulder hitting the sailor in the midriff. The man was following through with his punch, and, missing, was jackknifed over Luke's shoulder. His face smacked the edge of the wooden counter, breaking his nose. Luke came up at that same instant, his hands around the sailor's legs; he heaved the man over him.

The sailor's body cartwheeled over the counter and slammed into the dish racks behind it.

The four remaining seamen left their chairs at the same time and made a rush for the big Ranger braced against the counter.

The counterman had dropped to the floor and was scurrying on hands and knees toward the kitchen's swinging door, howling for help. The two noncombatant customers made a break for the outside door. . . .

The four sailors off the *Port of Call* hit Luke like a comber slapping up against a rock. The savage flurry lasted less than sixty seconds. Luke planted his boot into the stomach of one man and catapulted him across the narrow lunchroom. The sailor hit the opposite wall with his shoulders and the back of his head and lost all interest in the fight. Another pinwheeled over the counter to join the recumbent initiator of the fracas. The third man fell across an empty stool and curled over it like a very tired man.

The fourth combatant, a tall, bony, red-necked gladiator, stumbled away from Riatt, a dazed look on his bloody face. He brushed up against Remington Drake, who reached out and joyfully broke a bottle of ketchup across the man's head.

The next few moments were disconcertingly quiet. The counterman had stopped yelling. The last tinkle of breaking crockery had faded.

Slowly, with vast puzzlement in his owlish eyes, the counterman raised his head above the wooden surface. He put his palms on the counter and leaned over to survey the recumbent figures strewn about the lunchroom.

Luke pushed his empty coffee mug toward the man. "We'll have more coffee," he said. He wasn't even breathing hard.

The counterman gulped. He reached for the pot, moving over to refill Drake's. Carl Drake's brother had a wide grin on his bruised face. It was a gray and windy morning, but he had never enjoyed a pleasanter one.

They drank their coffee in peace. Luke stood up and dropped silver on the counter.

"Reckon the Navy will stand the damages," he told the open-mouthed man still holding the coffeepot in his hand. He turned to Drake. "Through? Let's go."

They walked back to the Curio Shoppe. It was a narrow-fronted, three-story building separated from the structure next to it by a narrow alley boarded off from the Avenue.

The shades were up, but the shop still looked closed. Luke tried the door, found it unlocked; he and Remington Drake walked in.

A bell sounded somewhere in the back of the shop, muted by distance and closed doors. Riatt glanced at items crowding the walls. Behind him young Drake murmured: "A nice little heap of second hand junk. . . ."

A door opened upstairs, and a stout, heavy-bosomed woman in her early fifties came down and paused on the landing visible from the store. Her left hand rested on the low railing. "Yes, *messieurs?*" Her tone was short and somewhat unfriendly.

Riatt was examining the trinkets in the show window. He turned and looked up at her, his smile pleasant. "We're looking for a cat. A small black cat about so high—" He measured it with his hands. "Green jade eyes and a kind of sassy smile."

The woman stood silent while the clocks on the walls ticked loudly. After a long pause she said: "I do not know what it is you are after, *monsieur.*"

"A friend of mine said he bought such a cat here," Luke persisted.

The woman frowned. "*Mon Dieu!* I sell many things here! It is possible. But I have no memory of such an object."

Drake had drifted toward the landing. He

looked up at Therese, his manner courteous. "I had the pleasure of meeting your stepdaughter, Justine, last night. I would like to see her again, if I may, Madame. Is she at home?"

The older woman's mouth tightened harshly. "You must be mistaken, *monsieur*," she said coldly. "I am Madame Monet. I have a step-daughter, yes. Her name is Justine. But she left Lafitte yesterday morning—to visit relatives in New Orleans."

Rem Drake glanced quickly at Luke, then back to Madame Monet. "But I saw your step-daughter last night," he insisted. "She seemed—well, she seemed as if she were trying to run away from—"

Madame Monet's voice cut sharply across his. "You were mistaken! Justine left yesterday morning, as I have said! It is quite possible you saw someone else."

She turned to look at the door as the bell sounded upstairs.

A small old man with bright black eyes walked in. He leaned on a silver-headed cane and he walked a little stiffly. A black cape, somewhat soiled, hung from his narrow shoulders.

The woman came down to meet him. He stopped, looking questioningly at Luke and young Drake. "Therese," he said quickly, "I am in no hurry. If these gentlemen are waiting to be served—?"

Therese said crossly: "I think they are more interested in asking foolish questions, *Monsieur* LeCoste." She threw her arms apart in an impatient gesture. "They came looking for a black cat in my shop!"

"A black cat?" The old man's mouth made a small O of puzzlement. Then his eyes sharpened. "But *oui,* Madame Monet—the black cat!" He turned to Luke Riatt. "A little statue, so high, of a black cat. No? Do you wish to buy it?"

Luke nodded. "Sounds like what we came after," he said dryly.

The old man rubbed the backs of his hands, and it sounded like the grating of fine sandpaper. "I have more, *monsieur*—a dozen more." He swung around to the woman. "Why did you not tell them?"

The woman shrugged. "I did not remember."

LeCoste snorted. "Therese, I am insulted!" He turned, his black eyes snapping at Riatt. "I am an *artiste, monsieur.* A fine *artiste!* Not with the paint brush—no! With clay—on the potter's wheel. Once a week, *monsieur,* I come to town and bring my masterpieces to Therese. She sells them for me, in this shop." He made a sweeping gesture with his left hand. "Here, among these—these—" He shrugged resignedly. "Ah, it is a living, *monsieur, n'est-ce-pas?*"

Luke nodded. He was trying to fit this old, somewhat eccentric figure into the grim pattern of smuggled jewels and murder.

"If you are interested, *monsieur*," LeCoste pressed eagerly, "I can get you this black cat. Two, perhaps? By this evening—"

Luke interrupted him. "If it's exactly like the one my friend has, the one which was in the window yesterday, I will buy it."

LeCoste rubbed his hands together avidly. "It will be. The exact same replica." He turned to the woman, standing apart, watching them with seeming indifference. "See? I have told you, Therese—the black cat is a masterpiece! I knew it when I turned it out on my potter's wheel. Now will you believe me when I say you should ask more than five dollars?" He cut himself short, bowing apologetically to the big Ranger. "You must forgive my excitement, *monsieur.* For you, of course, the price will remain the same. Five dollars—no?"

Luke said: "Sounds like a fair price." He turned to Drake. "You see—you must have been mistaken about the lady's stepdaughter."

Rem Drake took his cue reluctantly. "Of course," he muttered. He nodded to Madame Monet. "My apologies if I appeared rude, Madame."

They went out, the little bell jingling softly, muted by the closed door upstairs. Jules LeCoste waited, his right hand gripped tight over the silver head of his walking stick.

"They know!" the woman breathed.

"Too much!" LeCoste snapped. "The big one —he is a Texas Ranger! He is called Luke Riatt!"

The woman's shoulders slumped. "Everything appears to have gone wrong, Jules."

"Not everything!" the old man denied sharply. "I have recovered the black cat!" He sneered, his gaze lifting past this woman to the door which had just closed behind Riatt. "Even the Rangers can be foolish, Therese! Last night he left the cat in his saddle bag while he went up to his room in The Pierre House."

Therese said: "And Justine?"

"Etienne arrived safely with her. There is little danger she will try to run away again. We have only the one boat, and I myself came to Lafitte in it. Etienne remained on the island. He is a faithful watchdog."

"She will not be harmed, Jules?"

He shrugged. "If she gives Etienne no trouble."

Therese's thick hand closed over his thin, veined fist. "Jules! We have waited these many years, with a fortune we dared not claim as our own. I have grown old—I have watched you grow old! I—who had been one of the loveliest ladies-in-waiting to the Empress Carlotta—now I no longer look into the mirror!"

"I know," he said softly. He was still looking at the door, but his eyes were clouded with the warm memories of this woman as she had been thirty years past.

"We have disposed of her jewels at last," Therese continued. "We have riches enough—"

"No—not all of them!" Jules reminded her coldly.

"Enough to give us the wealth we sought," she pressed. "More than we can use, now." Her voice held a sharp anxiety. "Let us take what money we have and leave this place. The schooner is in the cove, Jules!" Her voice lifted hopefully. "I have promised Justine. Perhaps we can obtain passage to Vera Cruz—or wherever it goes—it will not matter."

He shook his head. "Not now, Therese. I will not flee because a Texas Ranger has arrived in town. I still have the cat—the last of Carlotta's jewels! When I have received payment for them —then, Therese, we will leave. And no one, not even the Ranger who calls himself Luke Riatt, will stop us!"

His fist taloned over the silver knob, blue veins popping on the back of his hands. "I have killed five men since the day that first customs officer walked in here asking for the cat. The Ranger Riatt may well be the sixth, Therese!"

CHAPTER EIGHT

— The Fortune Wheel —

Fifty feet below the gambling house known as the Fortune Wheel, the sea ran heavy, breaking against the weed-slick rocks at the base of the bluff. By noon the wind had died down, but a ground swell rolled in across the cove.

From the window of Lolita's room on the third floor, Gosh Jenkins watched the schooner, *Port of Call,* roll with the sea. He stood in front of the window, blotting out most of the gray day, an unlighted cigar between his teeth.

He was thinking of Luke Riatt.

Behind him the girl smudged out her cigaret in a clay ash tray on her dresser. Her black, sloe-shaped eyes hinted of an Oriental strain in a blood line predominantly Mexican. She stood five feet four—almost as tall as the constable—but she looked as fragile as a china doll in contrast. A vivid brunette, blooming early, she had come away from the squalor of a one-room adobe crowded with ten other children to applause and attention and a degree of wealth her parents had never envisioned. Lolita, at fifteen, sixteen and seventeen, had been the toast of New Orleans—of Natchez-on-the-Mississippi.

At twenty-five age had caught up with her. She was having trouble keeping her waist trim, and no application of paint and powder entirely erased the ravages of the past ten years from around her mouth and eyes.

"Why must I be it?" she asked nervously. She juggled the English language in a manner men found amusing, and she had never bothered to destroy this illusion by learning to speak correctly.

"I don't like it!" she pouted.

"You don't have to like it!" Jenkins growled. His voice was impatient. He turned and looked hard at her. "You just get him up here. I'll handle him myself this time."

Lolita's brows arched. "The Texas Rangers! They are *malo hombres,* Gosh! Even in my country it is said—"

Jenkins cut in harshly, nodding: "He's tough, all right, and strong. They say, Lolita, that he has never been beaten, by a faster gun—or a harder fist!" The big constable's lips pursed. "I'm going to prove that talk wrong!"

The Fortune Wheel entertainer turned back to her dresser and reached into a silver-lidded box for a tailor-made cigaret. She lighted it with nervous fingers.

"When I do it?"

"He'll be around," Jenkins replied. "Sooner or later he'll come in here."

She nodded. Her eyes were moody. "You queet, eh, after he is—" She groped for a word, settled for an expressive gesture. She walked to Jenkins, her smile softening, and draped her arm intimately around his thick neck. "You have *mucho dinero* now, no? Lolita knows. Thees buildin'—he is yours. Madame Paquet, she say eet ees hers—she ees boss. But I know. You are the beeg *patrone*—"

He flung her arm away from him. "You pry too much, Lolita!" he said coldly. He walked to the door and closed it behind him without looking back.

Lolita looked after him, her eyes hardening, her mouth turning bitter. . . .

Lou Gibbs, the faro dealer, was standing by his table, flicking cards from the top of a deck, when Jenkins came into the big downstairs gambling hall. Lou was a thin, jittery man who suffered from insomnia.

Except for the old man swabbing the floor in a corner, the gaming room was empty. Myles Hegstrom was standing alone at the rail of the long bar when Jenkins walked into the smaller room. Jenkins had been expecting the Open A boss. He joined Myles at the rail and nodded at the bartender's gesture. "Same." He waited until he was served, then downed the whiskey in one quick gulp. He didn't like whiskey—any hard liquor. But he drank it because Hegstrom did—and what any man did Jenkins would do better!

Hegstrom muttered into his glass: "My men are getting restless, Gosh. They've had enough of Lafitte."

Jenkins was staring down at the rail. "I saw Jules this morning," he said quietly. "He got the cat back."

Myles looked up, relief showing on his face. "Then I can pull out of here tonight?"

The constable shrugged. "This one will cost you fifty thousand, Myles!"

Hegstrom jerked around to face him. "Fifty thou—" He shook his head angrily. "You're crazy!"

"They're the last of the lot," Jenkins said, unmoved. "Jules says you'll get eighty-five—and the man who takes them off your hands will still make out with plenty."

The trail boss licked his lips. "I only brought thirty thousand dollars with me!"

"It's fifty!" Jenkins said inflexibly.

Hegstrom's mouth tightened. "I don't have it!"

"You sold six hundred head of beef here two days ago," Jenkins reminded him. "At twenty-one dollars per, it makes another twelve thousand!"

Hegstrom's laugh cut him short. "That money is not part of the deal we made. That's legitimate business—"

"How legitimate?" Jenkins demanded roughly. "I remember the day you trailed one hundred mangy-looking longhorn steers down to the docks. You had four out-at-the-elbows trail hands with you. Now you ship six hundred head of good beef and you pay wages to eight or ten men. That money, and that outfit you've got up north, didn't all come from raising beef, Myles!"

Hegstrom's voice rose angrily. "You haven't done so badly, either, Gosh!"

"I'm not complaining!" Jenkins snapped. He pushed his glass to the barman waiting discreetly at the far end of the counter, and waited until it was refilled. He added coldly: "Fifty thousand, Myles. This is the last batch. We don't even have to know each other after this."

Hegstrom shrugged resignedly. "Forty-five. It's all I can scrape together here." He added, not too convincingly: "I'll mail you the other five thousand."

Jenkins nodded. "All right. We'll wait for the rest of it."

The Open A boss finished his whiskey, scowling into the bottom of his glass. "I have to take your word that this one is worth that much, Gosh. Heck, I don't even know what's inside that cat."

"My word's been good on the others, Myles!"

Hegstrom pushed his empty glass away. "All right. When will I get it?"

"You've got the money with you?"

"No! It's in a strongbox, back at the chuck wagon!"

Jenkins' lips took on a cynical twist. "I'll get the cat from Jules this afternoon. I'll be at your camp tonight. In case anyone in town gets too curious and checks on me, I'm riding out on an official visit. I'm checking on Tully and Slim for my report to the sheriff's office."

Hegstrom nodded. Then: "That big Ranger—Luke Riatt. He still nosing around?"

Jenkins took the soggy end of his cigar from between his lips and eyed it for a long moment, not answering Myles. Then he dropped it deliberately into the brass cuspidor at his feet. His icy blue eyes met Hegstrom's as he said flatly: "Luke Riatt will be dead when I ride out to your camp tonight, Myles! You have my word on it!"

Hegstrom started to say something, changed his mind. He took change out of his pocket and dropped it on the counter. "I'll wait for you at French Creek, Gosh. Good luck."

The constable put his hand on Hegstrom's shoulder as the Open A boss started to turn. "Wait until I'm gone," he said quietly. "It'll look better."

He took another cigar from his coat pocket and lighted up. Then he walked out of the bar. The day had warmed up slightly, and it looked as though the sun would break through the overcast. He headed up the street, moving with easy, deliberate stride.

Two men rounded the corner of Orleans Avenue and headed his way. Jenkins didn't break stride. The tall, wide-shouldered man was Luke Riatt. He had never laid eyes on the younger, slender man with the Ranger. . . .

Jenkins nodded a greeting as they met. "Hi—Smith." He looked sharply at the cut on Luke's upper lip and the bruises on Drake's face and connected them with the fight in the lunchroom.

"Heard about the fracas in the Sea Urchin," he began. "I walked in about ten minutes after it happened." He grinned. "Just in time to hear how it started and to help Marvy Jones collect damages."

Luke said quietly: "Glad they settled the bill, Gosh." He nodded at the youngster at his side. "Meet Remington Drake. He's Carl Drake's brother." To young Drake: "Gosh Jenkins—town constable."

Jenkins smothered his surprise, allowing only a small measure of it to show in his voice. "Drake, eh?" He chuckled. "You here to check up on my story, too?"

Rem Drake nodded stiffly. "With no disrespect to you, Constable. But I know my brother didn't—"

"You've never met Lolita, son," the lawman

interrupted dryly. "But go right ahead, boy. I'm only a town constable. If the Rangers think there's more going on in Lafitte than I do, why, heck—who am I to question it?" He grinned mockingly. "Let me know what you find out, Luke."

Riatt was frowning thoughtfully as Jenkins walked on, turning left at the corner. Drake whistled with subdued respect. "He looked solid enough to derail the T & P long-haul engine, Luke. And he doesn't strike me as being as stupid as he likes to make out!"

Luke nodded thoughtfully. "He looks like the kind of man who won't admit he's wrong," he muttered. "That might explain a lot of things. But I'm beginning to wonder about him. . . ."

Drake uttered his own suspicions. "I wasn't wrong last night. That girl I picked up in the street was Justine. And she was hurt and scared, and she was running when I ran across her!" He reached up and felt of the tender lump at the back of his head. "Whoever slugged me must have been out looking for her. That's why Justine was running." He paused to look back down the street. "She knew something about my brother. If I could find her—"

The scene he had glimpsed from his window in the early morning hours suddenly flashed back into Riatt's mind. A girl in the bow of a small white skiff manned by a huge Negro—headed, he was sure, for the island at the mouth of the cove.

He told young Drake about it. Rem's eyes lighted up. "That must have been Justine! But what the devil! What's out on that island, anyway?"

"An old fort said to have been built by Lafitte, the pirate," Luke answered. "But I've got a hunch I want to follow through. Why don't you find out, maybe by checking at the Curio Shoppe again, where that old potter we met in there lives? I'm going to be doing a little checking myself—in the Fortune Wheel."

As young Drake started to wheel away: "Meet me there in an hour. . . ."

CHAPTER NINE

— Two On The House —

Jenkins pushed open the door of his office and walked inside. He started for his desk, then, warned by a strange prickling through the short hair on his neck, he whirled, his gun hand jerking at his Colt.

He came close to pulling trigger, so close it shook him with thin, savage anger. "Some day I'll shoot first, Jules!" he muttered harshly. "I'll regret it—but it won't do you any good!"

The old potter smiled coldly, unaffected by the huge man's outburst. He reached out with the tip of his walking stick and shoved the office door closed.

"You should spend less time in the Fortune Wheel and more in your office," he said quietly. He arched his gray brows in mock chiding. "People in Lafitte may begin to talk."

"Not in my hearing," Gosh growled. He shoved his Colt back into the holster, tossed his hat on a rack.

"I had a talk with Myles. He balked at paying fifty thousand—"

"Balked?" The old man turned on Gosh, his wiry body stiff, his voice icy. "I set the price! It

is not for him to decide to pay it—or refuse!"

Jenkins shrugged. "He's running scared, Jules."

"He's running fat!" Jules snapped back. He turned to look out through the dirty window, his mind reaching back into time to the years of planning, of waiting. Then he turned back to face Jenkins.

"He has grown rich, with the least risk. Now, at the first signs of trouble, he wants to back out?"

Jenkins shook his head. "I didn't say that; just that he didn't have fifty thousand dollars with him." He shrugged. "We didn't tell him how much to bring, Jules."

"He should have come prepared," the old man said. He took in a deep breath. "They are the last of them. Did you tell him? Worth at least eighty-five thousand."

"I told him," Gosh replied. "He promised to come up with forty-five thousand. He'll mail us the rest when he gets back."

Jules sneered. "You believe him?"

"I figure we have to," Jenkins said levelly.

Jules studied him for a long moment. The big man seemed resigned to accepting this, but Jules knew Jenkins better than that. There was something going on in the constable's mind— some plans of his own. He stifled his own inner anger. What right had he to expect more? If a man dipped his hand among thieves, could he

113

expect honesty? His smile was a thin, utterly mirthless grimace as he nodded slowly.

"When will he have the money?"

"I'm to bring the cat to him tonight at his camp on French Creek." Jenkins eyed Jules with disarming guilelessness. "He has the money hidden there, in the chuck wagon."

Jules frowned. "I'll fetch the cat—meet you back here before suppertime." He walked to the door, but paused; he looked back at Jenkins.

"I shall come with you," he said abruptly.

Jenkins hid his displeasure well. He shrugged.

"If you fancy a long ride, Jules, come ahead. But there's no need. I can handle Myles—"

"I was thinking of the Ranger, Riatt," Jules said coldly.

Jenkins' smile remained fixed on his face, like the smile painted on a cherub's face in a Bellini painting. "The Ranger will be dead before you return, Jules," he said quietly, "a victim of Lolita's charms and an admirer's jealousy."

Jules shook his head. "The ruse will not work this time, Gosh. Not even if she was Helen of Troy would the sheriff believe—"

"That will be my problem," Jenkins cut in flatly. "Anyway, by the time someone else comes nosing around, you'll be long gone, won't you?"

Jules nodded slowly. "It will be your neck," he said softly. Then, as the afterthought caught up with him: "Who will kill him? You?"

Jenkins said with quiet viciousness: "He is a strong man, Jules. But I will kill him—" he raised his hands in front of him—"with these!"

Jules was quiet for a long moment. Then: "Some day you will outmatch yourself, Gosh. I hope I am not here when it happens."

He turned as Jenkins grinned bleakly, opened the door. The constable watched the old man go out; then he let his hands drop by his sides again.

He was picking up forty-five thousand dollars from Myles Hegstrom that night. But this was one transaction he was not planning to turn over to Jules LeCoste!

This was his commission, for his part in the three-cornered deal, and Jules LeCoste would be in no position to argue when he found out!

Myles Hegstrom was finishing his last drink, preparatory to riding back to his camp, when Luke walked into the Fortune Wheel bar. His face was flushed from whiskey. He tossed a silver dollar on the counter as a tip and slipped his gold watch from his vest pocket to glance at the time.

Luke said pleasantly: "Still looking for a hand to replace Brenner, Mister Hegstrom?"

Hegstrom whirled. His eyes had a startled, trapped look that lasted only a fleeting moment. Then he nodded, his tone cautious. "I could use a good man," he admitted.

"I've decided to take you up on your offer," Luke said seriously. "Where do I join your outfit?"

Hegstrom said quickly: "We're pulling out tonight."

"I'll leave with you," Luke said. "I've had all I can stand of this town." He waited for Myles to speak, then asked again: "Where did you say you were camped?"

Hegstrom was trapped. He licked his lips. "Out by French Creek, about seven miles west of town."

Luke nodded. "Let me buy you a drink, boss."

Hegstrom shook his head. "I've had more than my quota for the day, Smith." He walked out, cursing silently. Darn Jenkins! The big constable had better make sure the Ranger didn't come out to French Creek tonight!

Luke Riatt breasted the bar, felt in his pockets for change, palmed it on the counter. "Double or nothing," he suggested to the waiting bartender.

"I'll do better than that." The bald-headed barman grinned. He had yellow stubs for teeth. He turned and indicated a big wheel on the wall behind him. The wheel was set on a small iron axle, allowing it to spin freely. The rim was boxed off into red and black numbers from one to ten, repeated several times. The red and black numbers alternated on the wheel.

"Take yore pick, red or black. I spin the wheel.

Number on yore color choice comes up, I hand you that many free drinks. House color comes up, you pay me for the drinks you don't get. Fair enough?"

Luke shrugged. "Spin her."

The wheel stopped with the pointer at red two. The barman said cheerfully: "Two on the house. What'll it be, stranger?"

"Whiskey—your brand." Luke watched the bartender pour. "I reckon this is why it's called the Fortune Wheel," he said, making conversation. "Who owns the place?"

"Madame Paquet," the barman said. "Took over when her husband died a few years back. I wasn't working here then." He wiped the bar under Luke's elbow with a damp cloth. "Best gambling house west of New Orleans," he boasted. "Too early for business yet. But," he smirked, "we've got the best entertainers west of the Mississippi." He leaned over the bar, his voice dropping an octave, becoming confidential. "They live upstairs. You're new here, I see. Then you'll want a treat. Come back around ten tonight to see Lolita dance."

"She good?"

"Good?" The barman made a weak gesture indicating his astonishment at Luke's question. "Stick around and see for yourself—" He cut himself off, his eyes widening. "Well, I'll be—" he began again, lowering his voice and point-

ing. "She never gets up this early—but, here comes Lolita now!"

Luke turned. The girl coming through the archway into the bar wore a sheath-tight blue dress with a slit at the left that revealed a long length of brown leg as she walked. The neckline plunged, revealing enough to Luke so that he understood what drew customers to the Fortune Wheel. Her face, the color of half-and-half coffee, was a little too round. Her lips were made up too pouting. Her black eyes were a bit too slanted to strike more than a passing chord in the big Ranger. But she was undeniably attractive, even in the harsh light of day.

Lolita came to the bar, her steps quick and nervous. "Wheesky! Beeg one, Jerry!"

The barman poured. Lolita picked up the glass, touched her lips to it, spat it out. "Ugh! No, no, Jerry! Not thees—the brand special. The bottle Madame Paquet, the wheesky she keep for special company, *si!* "

Jerry's eyes blinked. "Oh, yeah?" He glanced around the bar like a conspirator about to indulge in a bit of petty thievery. "Well, guess Mrs. Paquet won't miss a short one, Lolita." He ducked under the counter.

Lolita turned to Luke, fumbling a cigaret out of her bag. "You have the light, *monsieur?*"

Luke found and struck a match for her cigaret. Lolita appeared nervous. Her eyes were wide, her pupils dilated. She sucked in a deep inhalation of smoke. *"Gracias, senor,"* she said.

Luke grinned faintly. Lolita was also multilingual, he noticed, although her conversation was hard to follow in any language. Still, she didn't have to talk too much to make herself understood.

The bartender poured Lolita's drink from a dark green bottle with a French label. The girl said: "A dreenk for my very good *amigo*—" She turned to Luke expectantly, smiling invitingly at him.

"Smith," Luke said evenly.

"For Smeeth," she repeated.

The bartender poured. "I'll join you in this one," he said quickly, leaning halfway over the bar to keep his voice down. He glanced quickly at the door again, as if expecting to see someone enter. "Wouldn't want Mrs. Paquet to catch me handing out her special brand like this. But," he grinned slyly, "let's bottoms-up on this one, Smith."

Luke smiled. "Well, here's to—" He turned to Lolita. "To the best little entertainer east *or* west of the Mississippi," he toasted. He lifted his glass to his lips and tossed the whiskey down. He knew what had happened before it reached his stomach. He dropped the glass on the brass rail, reached under his coat and rested the long muzzle of his Colt on the bar edge.

"Spin that wheel, Baldy!" he said grimly. "Before it stops I want you to tell me who put you up to it!"

The bartender shrank back from that deadly muzzle. "I—Cripes, Smith—I don't know what's riled you."

Luke took a deep breath, trying to clear the fog creeping into his head. "You know what's riling me, Baldy! Madame Paquet's special brand," he said thickly. He knew then that he wouldn't make it. "Doped whiskey." The words seemed to come reluctantly through his teeth. "Who—put—you—up—to?"

Out of the corners of his eyes Luke saw the girl move. He turned, feeling the drug clog his muscles, hearing a low roaring build up in his ears. Lolita had the whiskey bottle in her hand, raised to strike at him. Luke gripped her wrist as she lunged at him, and the bottle jerked out of his fingers. It broke on the bar, spilling liquor and glass fragments across the counter.

Jerry had ducked below the counter. Luke's vision was blurring. He shoved the girl away from him, turned toward the outside door. "Reckon this is how—Bert Morse—and Carl Drake—were—"

He didn't finish. The blackness came up and blotted out the sight of the girl staring at him. He fell heavily, but he did not feel the impact of the fall. . . .

CHAPTER TEN

— Island Trap —

Dark clouds began to mass on the horizon for another assault on Lafitte. A bell rang four times on the *Port of Call*, and the rising wind carried the sound to Remington Drake as he was retracing his steps to the Curio Shoppe.

The small caped figure of Jules LeCoste, turning down a narrow side street to the waterfront, caught Drake's eye. He hesitated only a moment. The old man was probably going home, in which case it would save him time if he followed LeCoste right to his place of business.

The alley, labeled Cove Road, dipped down rather steeply to the shacks clustered along the shore. Drake followed at a distance, but the old man didn't look back once. He headed directly for a small shack on the water. A rickety wooden jetty ran twenty feet out into the cove. Several small boats were tied up alongside. One of them was a white-painted skiff.

The old man disappeared into the shack. He came out almost immediately, a squat man by his side. The man looked at the forming weather, studied it for a moment, then started to shake his head. LeCoste handed out some bills to the

121

man, who stuffed them into his pocket.

They got into the white skiff together, the old potter moving up to a seat at the bow. The squat man took his place at the oars. He pushed the skiff away from the jetty, nosed it seaward and dug in the oars.

Drake waited until he was sure of their destination: the island across the cove. He was pretty sure now that the girl Luke Riatt had seen that morning had been Justine; that she had been taken prisoner after he had been knocked unconscious and transported to the island, where she was being held and couldn't talk.

Drake felt a strong urge to follow the old man to the island. But he had promised the Ranger he'd meet him. He turned back reluctantly to the gambling hall.

The *Fortune Wheel* was still deserted when he pushed through the door and walked to the bar. The bald-headed, pouchy-eyed bartender jerked nervously when he heard the door open, raising startled eyes to Drake. He lowered them almost immediately and quickly found something to do at the far end of the counter.

A big-bosomed redhead in a green, flouncy dress was drooped over the bar. She lifted her head and studied Rem Drake as he came up alongside; her eyes had a sickly wet gleam. Her smile of greeting was automatic, but her heart was not in it. She turned around to face the bartender, her voice doleful. "Quick, Jerry," she pleaded, "before my head rolls off."

The bartender mixed Seidlitz powders in a glass of water and pushed it toward her. The redhead groaned, but drained the fizzing mixture.

The bartender now turned his attention to Drake, who said casually: "I'm looking for a big feller named Smith. He promised to meet me in here."

The bartender shrugged. "A big hombre walked in here a while back," he recalled indifferently. "Had two drinks on the house and said he'd be back tonight, when the place was more lively."

Drake frowned. Riatt had probably gone back to the hotel. He ordered a drink and, as the bartender poured, asked: "Anyone live out on that island across the cove?"

The barman shook his head. But the redhead contradicted him. "Sure," she said. The sick look was disappearing from her eyes. "Some old coot named LeCoste lives in the old fort. Makes pottery for a living."

She glanced quickly at the barman as he shoved a drink toward her. "On the house, Madge," the bartender said. "Helps chase away the morning after blues."

Drake finished his drink and paid for it. "I'll be back later," he said. "If that big feller, Smith, comes in here, tell him I was looking for him."

The bartender nodded. Madge picked up her

drink, eyeing the bald-headed man with a belli-
cose stare. The bartender muttered something
under his breath as he moved away. . . .

Remington Drake walked quickly back to the
waterfront. The rain clouds were almost overhead, and he knew he'd have to move fast if he
wanted to reach LeCoste's place before the new
storm broke. The island was less than two miles
out.

He checked along the small wharfs until he
found a boat for rent. The man took his money
and handed him a pair of oars. He untied the
skiff, shoved it away from the wharf and stood
for a few moments staring as Drake, not too
familiar with a boat, had trouble with the oars
before settling down to a steady but erratic
course. The boat's owner looked up at the darkening sky, then tightened his fingers over the
money Drake had given him. Even if he lost
the ancient skiff, he was still money ahead. He
shook his head slowly and went back to the
shelter of his shack.

Remington rowed steadily. He felt the drag of
the sea as it ran toward the cove shore; the
rising wind whistled coldly about his ears. It
bit through his thin coat, making him wish he
had taken time to get into something warmer.

The skiff's prow chopped steadily into the
waves; they were forming whitecaps on either

side of him. His shoulders ached. Twice he snagged an oar and sprawled back into the boat; the skiff started to yaw. A small wave hit it broadside, and the boat shipped water. With a desperate effort Remington refitted the oar into its oarlock. He worked it savagely, slowly nosing the prow around into the waves. He glanced over his shoulder to line himself up with the island.

He was a bitter, exhausted man when he finally pulled up in the lee of the island. The water calmed here, and he felt the pressure of the wind ease against his back. He dug in with dogged determination; then, glancing over his shoulder and finding the island shoreline only a few yards away, he shipped his oars and slumped tiredly, letting momentum bring him in.

He felt the prow grate softly against sand, and he roused. The boat rocked as he headed for the bow, grabbed the coiled anchor rope and jumped ashore. He landed in four inches of water and ran up the beach, looking for something to tie the boat to. An old ship's timber, most of it buried in the sand, provided mooring. He tied the skiff securely, then glanced toward the small rock jetty farther down the beach.

LeCoste's skiff, painted a weathered green, rode at anchor alongside the jetty. The white skiff that had brought LeCoste there was gone. The seaman who had rowed the old man out there must have returned immediately to Lafitte.

Remington Drake glanced at his still half clenched hands. The oars had left deep red marks in his palms, and several blisters had formed on the pads of his fingers. He smiled ruefully. A man toughened his wits at cards, but it did little for his hands. Of course, they developed a certain manual dexterity. . . .

He took a deep breath as the first pelting drops chilled his face. The pistol in his shoulder holster felt reassuring. He started to walk toward the jetty and the small path which led from it to the old stone fort he saw beyond it. . . .

Etienne, roaming the small island like a watchdog, had watched the slow, erratic course of Drake's skiff as it headed for the island. He had squatted behind screening brush, his eyes following the boat. Now they held on Drake as he started up the path to the old stone fort.

The fringe of the squall coming in from the sea ran its pelting drops across the island, making soft, scurrying sounds in the brush and across the sand. Etienne waited, silent and immovable. Remington Drake passed by less than twenty feet from him and did not notice the big Negro.

Slowly Etienne reached for the hunting knife in a sheath at his belt. He straightened slowly, like some big black cat, his eyes following Drake's progress.

Drake came up to the heavy door of the stone fort and paused, his hand sliding into his coat for his shoulder gun. He glanced around in wary reconnaissance, then reached for the iron latch. . . .

A savage gust of wind and rain pelted him, pushing him roughly against the door. At almost the same instant Etienne's thrown knife slammed into him, the blade biting deep, deflected upward by the wide flat bone of his shoulder blade.

He fell against the door, his left hand fumbling with the latch. He turned against it, his face to the wind and the rain. His pain-blurred eyes made out the big Negro bounding toward him and he tried to lift up his gun, his lips pulling back in a taut effort against his lips.

Etienne shied away from the muzzle blast, then came in on Drake, his big hand chopping at Drake's gun wrist. The gun dropped from Drake's numb hand. He raised it in an instinctive endeavor to ward off Etienne's coming blow, then felt himself falling backward, into the fort, as someone yanked the door open behind him.

He fell heavily down the three stone steps that led into the big room Jules LeCoste used as his shop. The impact jarred him unconscious.

Jules LeCoste stood over him, his glance lifting to the big Negro in the doorway. Rain slanted in through the open door. LeCoste made a quick motion. "Come inside. Close the door!"

Etienne obeyed.

Jules eyed Drake for a moment, pondering the man's fate. Behind him Justine came into the big room and stared at the unconscious youngster. Her frightened gasp made LeCoste turn to her.

"It is the same boy who was with you last night," Jules said coldly. "Who is he?"

Justine shook her head. "I don't know."

Jules made an imperious gesture with his hand, ordering her to his side. She hung back. Jules looked at Etienne, who turned immediately and started for her.

Justine brushed past him and went to Jules' side. Her face was white as she looked down at Drake.

"Who is he?" LeCoste repeated. His voice held a cruel insistence.

Justine licked her lips. "He said he was Carl Drake's brother."

Jules frowned. The news disturbed him, not so much because of any threat posed by this youngster, but because of a nagging uneasiness that things were getting out of hand. The law's credulity had been strained by Jenkins' explanation of the deaths of Carl Drake and Bert Morse; there would be no way to avoid accounting for the killings yesterday.

He turned to Justine, his voice harsh. "How

much did you tell him last night?"

Justine seemed to shrivel up inside. "Nothing." Her voice was small, frightened. "I was running away, as I told you. . . . I slipped and fell and hurt my ankle." She paused, biting her lips. "I told him nothing."

Jules turned to Etienne. "Bring him into the other room," he said harshly. "I'll decide what to do with him later."

CHAPTER ELEVEN

— "With My Bare Hands!" —

Luke Riatt regained consciousness slowly. His tongue felt thick in his mouth. He opened his eyes and found himself face down on the bed covers. He closed his eyes again and tried to remember what had happened to him. His mind worked slowly, as though pushing up through a mental fog.

A man's voice sounded flatly in his ears. "You'll live, Ranger!"

Riatt rolled over and sat up on the edge of the bed. His stomach heaved slightly and he fought back the nausea that came up in his throat. He surveyed the room, finding it strange —a fair-sized room and obviously a woman's room. A heavy perfume, jasmine, clung to the air. He closed his eyes again, trying to remember.

The man's grating voice said: "All right, Lolita. I'll take care of things now!"

Riatt opened his eyes again and turned to the voice. Gosh Jenkins was standing against the closed door, watching him with a peculiar smile. The girl who had offered him a drink at the bar downstairs was standing by his side. She had Luke's gun belt in her hand.

The sight of her cleared Luke's head. He stood up, his eyes squinting at the small, sharp pain that throbbed above his eyes. His gaze focused on Jenkins. The ponderous constable was unbuckling his gunbelt, adding it to Luke's in Lolita's arms.

"Leave them with Jerry, down at the bar," the constable instructed her. "I'll be down to pick them up later."

Lolita cast one white-faced glance at the Ranger, then sidled out. Jenkins slowly closed the door behind her.

Riatt smiled bleakly. He took a step away from the bed, glanced out of the single window. He found himself looking down a sheer seventy-foot drop to wet black rocks washed by the restless sea. His glance moved out and held for a long bitter moment on the man in a small boat, bucking the chop in the cove. It looked like young Drake, but he couldn't be sure. . . .

The constable's voice was harsh, mocking him with deadly seriousness. "That's the way you're going, Ranger! Out the window!" His laughter was short, ugly. "You can jump now and save me the trouble!"

Luke turned to face the man. Jenkins was locking the bedroom door with a key. He turned to face Luke, smiling, holding up the key for Luke. Then he thrust it deliberately and with grim meaning into his pocket.

"There are two ways out of this room, Luke," Jenkins said. "One is through that window. The other is behind me. But you'll have to get by me first!"

Riatt absorbed this slowly. He was still not functioning clearly—the throbbing in his head seemed to echo the faint nausea in his stomach. But Jenkins' stand cleared up a lot of things that had puzzled him. And it provided the answers he had come to Lafitte to find.

Jules LeCoste, Gosh Jenkins and Myles Hegstrom! They were linked together. And the Curio Shoppe and Lolita were but blinds in the pattern of smuggling that Morse and Carl Drake had come to investigate.

He noded grimly. "It makes a lot of sense now," he said bitterly. "It explains why Bert Morse and Carl Drake were killed in Lolita's room—this room! And it explains why your report was confirmed by the deputy sheriff."

Jenkins shrugged. "I am the law in Lafitte. Why should the deputy doubt my word?" He was taking his coat off as he talked, his eyes holding watchfully on Riatt. "I could have killed you while you were lying unconscious on the bed. My report then would have been like the others I sent out, and if Captain Hughes of the Rangers doubted it, I would provide witnesses to swear that the great Luke Riatt, too, succumbed to the charms of Lolita and was killed by a jealous suitor. If need be I would even provide the body of the murderer, like I provided Enrico for the killing of young Bert Morse!"

"Bert and Carl Drake were stabbed to death," Luke pointed out. He was stalling for time, waiting for the weakness in his knees to go away. His mouth still tasted as though it were full of cotton fuzz, and the small point of pain pressing behind his eyes was growing.

"I didn't kill *them!*" Jenkins replied heavily. He dropped his coat on a chair by the door and started rolling up his sleeves. His hairy fore-arms were like small logs. "That was Jules' idea. He likes to test out his sword—"

"The black cat!" Luke cut in bleakly, the puzzle coming together now. "Carlotta's jewels are in the black cat baked in the ovens of LeCoste. From LeCoste to the Curio Shoppe—but only the right man is allowed to buy the cat. Myles Hegstrom! That's the way it was worked, wasn't it?"

The constable's big hands came down slowly. "Yeah—that's the way it was. LeCoste had a fortune in jewels, but no way to get them into the country and to a buyer without tangling with the Federal government. LeCoste didn't feel like sharing what he had with anybody—"

"Mainly because those jewels weren't his!" Luke snapped. "So he decided to split them three ways—you, Hegstrom and his share!"

Jenkins sneered. "That's the way it turned out. But that's one report you'll never get back to Houston, Ranger. And when Captain Hughes sends another man down here, it'll be all over. The last of Carlotta's jewels are in the black cat Jules took from your saddle bag last night. By tomorrow Hegstrom will be on his way back with it!"

Riatt cast one quick glance out the window. Remington Drake was a small, indistinct figure on the bobbing boat pulling into the lee of the small island.

Jenkins' voice was cold. "I saw him, too—young Drake. The poor fool will never leave that island alive!"

Riatt turned, got his back up against the window and waited. Jenkins paused, eyeing him like a grizzly sizing up a cougar he had cornered. "No man ever did to me what you did back in my office," he said, rage thickening his voice. "For that, Riatt, I'm going to kill you with my bare hands!"

The Ranger timed himself to Jenkins' shuffle. He took a long step forward and slugged Jenkins with all he had. His right hand landed a little too high; he felt his knuckles give, and pain shot up his arm to his shoulder.

The constable's cheek split under the vicious impact. His face distorted briefly and for a moment he faltered, his knees buckling. Then he closed in, his thick arms wrapping ponderously around Luke's back. . . .

The enormous strength of the man came into play then. The big Ranger's back muscles corded, writhed, as he tried to break Jenkins' crushing grip. The constable buried his face under Luke's chin and threw his weight forward. The Ranger was momentarily helpless. His hands were free, but he had no target except Gosh Jenkins' powerful back, and the lawman's crushing grip was slowly cutting off his breathing!

Despite himself he was jammed back, and then he realized Jenkins' murderous intention. The window! At the last minute he twisted sideways. His shoulder hit the window; he was pushed partially through it, breaking the glass, and heard it jangle down on the sill and break down on the rocks below. Jenkins suddenly grunted. His crushing grip around Luke's waist momentarily relaxed, and the Ranger jammed both hands under Jenkins' arms and tore himself free.

He saw what had loosened the constable's grip as Jenkins wheeled, lifting his hands to close on Luke again. Jagged glass had gashed deep across the backs of his hands when he had shoved Riatt against the window!

The Ranger didn't give him another chance. Luke hit him twice as Jenkins groped for him—

sledgehammer blows that stopped the bulky man short and drove grunts of surprised pain from his battered lips.

Jenkins managed to close in just once more. One big hand clawed into Luke's face, slipped down and fastened on Riatt's throat. The other tried to sledge blows into Luke's stomach.

The Ranger worked both hands in a savage, brutal attack against Jenkins' unprotected stomach. Jenkins gasped. His hand dipped from Luke's throat and a dazed, frightened look spread across his blood-distorted features. He started to back away, and Luke Riatt went after him, his black-flecked eyes blazing like a tiger's.

"This the way you want it, Jenkins?" he sneered. His eyes were slitted, glittering with a wicked light. All the savage fury in the big Ranger had been touched off by Jenkins' rough handling of him, and each blow now smashed something in the hulking man backing away from him.

Jenkins cursed thickly. His nose was a flattened, bloody mess; his broken ribs brought pain into his slitted eyes. He fell back under Riatt's assault, no longer willing to grapple with this man. He clubbed out blindly, more to ward off Luke's terrible blows than to fight back. He kept backing up, staggering, pawing at Luke, until the door stopped him. Then he lunged forward, head lowered, and rammed Luke in the stomach.

Riatt fell back and tripped on a fold of the scuffed oval throw rug. He twisted like a cat and was up on his feet while Jenkins stood, dragging in welcome gulps of air.

The constable groped inside his pants pocket and came up with a wicked-looking switch-knife. The blade sprang out as he thumbed the catch.

"You're worse—than I expected—" he panted. He wiped blood from his eyes. "Didn't think—I'd have to—use this!" He lunged forward, knife held low at his side.

Luke waited until Jenkins' knife arm came up, slashing at his stomach. Then he clamped his right hand on Jenkins' thick wrist and jammed the lawman's hand back, using the heavy man's momentum as leverage. A bitter groan tore through Jenkins' clenched lips as Riatt swung in behind him and jerked savagely upward on his arm. A bone snapped, and the knife slid from Jenkins' fingers as pain tore a sharp cry from his lips.

He fell back, moving blindly, too hurt to see where he was going. He hit the partially demolished window, tried to regain his balance. The sashing gave way under his weight. He went through, his outcry short and terrible as he fell. . . .

Luke leaned his tired, aching body against the window frame and took in deep gulps of fresh air. Blood was blurring the vision in his right eye, and he wiped it with the back of his left hand. His right hand was stiffening, swelling. His throat was raw, and the marks of Jenkins' powerful fingers had left their red imprint.

There was a sudden hammering on the locked door. Someone called anxiously: "Jenkins! You all right?"

Riatt sneered. "Jenkins is in Hades!" he answered harshly.

There was a moment of stark, shocked silence beyond that locked door. The wind blew in through the broken window, and the first drops of rain came, scuttling like a horde of crabs across the rooftop. The patter reminded Luke that he was on the top floor of the Fortune Wheel—that only the flat roof was above him.

A bullet splintered through the door—another! Then a man's voice yelled: "Hold it, Sam! The door's locked. He can't get away!"

Luke walked to the dresser and shook the earthenware pitcher. Water slopped against its sides. He poured some into the enameled basin and washed the blood from his face. The fight had cleared his head.

From behind the locked door he heard steps. Then a voice snarled: "I'm gonna wait just five minutes. Then we go in after him!"

Luke stared bitterly at the door. Slowly he backed to the window, glanced down and out.

Waves sloshed over the slick black rocks below. Jenkins' body lay crumpled between two boulders. Small waves broke over him, jamming his body among the hemming rocks.

Luke's eyes held a trapped glitter. He had stopped Jenkins. But there was no way out of the room except through that bullet-scarred door. And from the whispered consultations that seemed to be going on, there were at least four or five armed men waiting for him in the corridor!

CHAPTER TWELVE

— The Confession —

The squall began battering the Fortune Wheel, the wind screaming high and wild off the Gulf. In the corridor outside Lolita's door the four men waited, guns drawn. Their anger was touched with caution.

Sam, a raw-boned hardcase with a patch over his left eye, paced restlessly. He couldn't believe Jenkins had gotten the worst of the fight in that room.

He paused, pressing in close to the wall next to the door. "Gosh," he called grimly, "you hurt?"

There was no answer from the room now. The rain beat hard on the roof; it sopped up what slight sound the big Ranger might have been making. Sam sucked in a harsh breath. Only a fool would try to get out through that window, he thought. . . .

He turned as Jerry, the bartender, came up the stairs. The bald-headed man halted on the stairs just below the landing; his eyes were on the level of Sam's knees.

He held up two gunbelts. "Belong to Jenkins— and the Ranger!" he whispered. He glanced at the door. "He ain't got a gun, Sam."

Sam nodded grimly and turned back to the door. Slowly he thumbed the hammer back on his Frontier model, lined it up with the lock. . . .

Inside Lolita's room, Luke heard whispering out in the corridor. He turned to the bed and picked up the pillow. Using it to shield his fist, he knocked the rest of the glass from the window. Then he stepped up on the sill, leaned out and looked up.

That flat roof was about a foot and a half above his outstretched hand. An easy jump, ordinarily. But from his position on the sill, any upward thrust would tend to throw him away from the edge of the roof.

He searched for a handhold, a projection, anything on the outside of the building that would provide momentary leverage while he jumped. But the wet clapboards provided no handhold.

He stepped back into the room, baffled.

On the other side of the locked door a voice said angrily: "The devil with it! Jerry says he ain't got no gun! I'm shooting my way inside!"

Luke stepped back as a slug splintered through the door and thunked into the far wall. His foot twisted as he stepped on something hard and he looked down. Jenkins' knife! He scooped it up and headed for the window as another bullet ripped through the door, splintering the lock. The lead slug whined off the bedpost!

Balanced on the sill, Luke held himself with

his left hand cupped against the upper part of the window framing. Jenkins' knife was gripped in his right hand. His fingers felt numb and as unwieldy as sausages. He set his teeth and forced his fingers to close over the bone handle.

Reaching over his head, he jammed the sharp blade into the wood!

The knife bit deep into the clapboarding. The Ranger tested it. It held firm.

The rain was pelting hard against his neck and shoulders. He didn't look down to the wave-pounded rocks below. One slip and he'd wind up with Gosh Jenkins.

He leaned out, gripping the knife handle with his left hand. His muscled body tensed. Then he jumped, keeping himself in toward the wall with his grip on the knife.

He felt it pull loose just as the fingers of his right hand caught the overhang! Pain knifed through his swollen knuckles. The knife slipped out of his left hand and went glinting down. For a moment he hung by one hand, dangling against the window. He swung his left hand up to join his right, and his shoulder muscles corded as he swung himself up and over.

The rain swept across the rooftop like a gray curtain. He didn't wait to get his breath. He ran toward the front of the gambling house, remembering that the two-decker porch would provide a way of exit from the roof.

The sloping, shingled roof of the porch lay six feet below him. He dropped to it, and found himself facing a partially opened window. It opened wider under the savage thrust of his hand.

The redheaded entertainer named Madge was standing in her doorway, looking down the hall. She turned as Luke came through the window. The big Ranger stopped short, eyeing her with grim expectancy.

"Which way down to the bar?" he asked coldly.

She eyed him without too much surprise. "Out this door and down the stairway on your left, mister."

Luke took three long steps across the room and stopped just inside the door. There seemed to be a commotion coming from the rear of the gambling hall.

He stared hard at her; she looked at him with cool speculation. Luke said dryly: "You *could* scream."

"I quit screaming long ago," the woman said. Her smile was cynical. "I don't owe them anything."

Luke shrugged. He started through the doorway and she put out a hand, momentarily holding him up. "I don't know who you are, big fellow. But I heard Jenkins locked the door on you and him in Lolita's room. That's where the commotion's coming from. What happened in there?"

"Jenkins' dead!" Luke answered brusquely.

He stepped past her, found the stairway leading down and took it.

The redhead leaned back against the door framing, her lips twisted with secret pleasure. "So Gosh finally grabbed a tiger by the tail," she murmured. The thought seemed to amuse her, but her eyes held a deep, enduring hurt. She had been in love with Jenkins, although the constable had never returned the emotion. She turned away, closing the door, walked slowly back to her dresser and groped for a cigaret. . . .

The bartender was craning his neck, looking through the archway into the gambling room, when Luke came downstairs. He had scurried down from the third floor as Sam had started firing, preferring to wait in the comparative safety of the bar while the others hunted for the big Ranger who had killed Jenkins.

His attention focused toward the stairs, he wasn't aware of Luke until the Ranger vaulted over the bar and landed three feet from him. He jerked around, banging his elbow against the back shelf, and his mouth dropped.

Luke said grimly: "I'll take back my cartridge belt and gun right now!"

Jerry gestured weakly to an undercounter shelf. Luke reached down, pulled his gunbelt out and buckled it about his waist. He shifted the weight of his holster until it was comfortable and was about to leave when his attention was directed elsewhere.

Lolita and two other girls, trailing behind three angry men, came through the archway, heading for the bar. A tall, turkey-necked man with a cast in his left eye was holding a gun in his hand. He didn't expect to see Riatt behind the bar, and his glance skidded off the Ranger, to Jerry standing like a petrified caricature farther down the counter.

"Hang it, Jerry!" the tall man growled. "The big feller got away—"

Luke's voice rapped across the room. "Not too far!" he corrected bleakly.

The house gambler jerked. He started to bring his Colt muzzle up, and fear tightened his trigger finger prematurely. His slug smashed into the counter baseboarding. Luke's bullet spun him three quarters around. He stood up for a short instant, blood darkening his shirt at his right shoulder. Then his knees buckled and he sat down, his face whitening.

The two men with him froze. Lolita glanced at Luke, reacted to the grim anger in his face, and started to back away toward the big gambling hall behind her.

Luke's Colt stopped her. He gestured with it, his invitation including all of them. But his eyes indicated that Lolita was his preferred guest.

"The drinks are on the house, gents. And the ladies, too!"

They came up, shuffling slowly, all except the man with the smashed shoulder.

Luke's voice was hard and as unyielding as coiled steel. "We'll settle one thing right now. I'm the law in Lafitte, until someone is appointed to take Gosh Jenkins' place!"

One of the men standing beside Lolita said sullenly: "You've got no right to—"

He stopped, swallowing hard. They all stared at the badge Luke held up for them to see.

"Luke Riatt," he bit out coldly. "Texas Ranger."

The sullen man licked his lips. "Mister, I ain't arguing with that badge!"

Luke turned his attention to Lolita. "Two men were killed in your room a few weeks ago. One of them, Carl Drake, had a wife and two children in Galveston. Just for the record, I want a written and witnessed account of how Carl got to your room, and why he was killed!"

Lolita nodded quickly. Jenkins was dead, and there was no point now to the deception. She stared at Jerry, and the bartender suddenly remembered that he kept paper and a pencil under the counter. He produced them.

Luke waited until the entertainer had finished her statement, had it witnessed by all present, and shoved the folded paper into his coat pocket. He put his left hand on the counter and

146

vaulted over it. The others crowded back, giving him room.

He pointed the muzzle of his gun at Jerry. "You see that Madame Paquet gets the word. The Fortune Wheel is closed as of right now! It will remain closed until a new constable is appointed!"

Jerry shrugged. "No need of that, Ranger!" He shrank back as Luke eyed him grimly. "There never was any Madame Paquet," he said quickly. "Gosh Jenkins owned this place." He made a gesture. "I guess Gosh figgered it would look better this way. He didn't want folks to start wonderin' how somebody livin' off a constable's pay could afford to buy a big place like this."

Luke nodded. "In that case, *you* lock up. There'll be an inquiry later, and a court will decide on the disposition of this place." He eyed the others with cold challenge. "Anyone object?"

No one did.

Luke Riatt walked out into a driving rain. He headed directly for the waterfront, remembering Jenkin's comment on young Drake. The rash youngster should have waited, he thought grimly.

He tried at the first boathouse he came to. A dark, heavy-set man was lying in a bunk, his shoes off, reading an old copy of the *Police Gazette*. A three-quarters-full bottle of cheap whiskey lay on the floor beside him.

Luke said: "I want to hire somebody to row me out to that island—"

The seaman sat up and shook his head. "Man, you must be crazy—"

He choked into abrupt silence as Luke's gun muzzled him.

"I haven't got time to argue!" the big Ranger said harshly.

The seaman eyed the gun muzzle; his jaw set stubbornly. "I'll let *you* have the boat, mister. But I ain't rowin' anybody anywhere. Not in this squall!"

Luke studied him for a bitter moment, then nodded grimly. "All right—let me have the boat!"

The seaman got up, slipped into a pair of boots and took down his slicker from a nail on the wall. He reached up for a pair of oars resting on pegs on the wall and handed them to Luke. Then he led the way outside, out to the creaking wooden jetty. The rain slashed at them, driving into Luke's face. He stared down at the bobbing skiff the seaman indicated.

"That's it, mister!" he muttered. He added under his breath. "I hope you kin swim!"

Luke stepped down into the rocking boat and fitted the oars into their oarlocks. The boat-house man untied the skiff and tossed the short length of rope into the bow. He reached down quickly and tossed a rusted quart can in after the rope. "You'll need it for bailing!" he yelled as Luke shoved clear of the pier and bent to the oars.

He waited a moment, suffering the discomfort of the driving rain in order to watch. "I don't know what you're after, big feller," he muttered. "But I'd hate to be it. I'd sooner be in that water and have a tiger shark come after me!"

The small boat was almost lost in the gray howling squall when he turned back to the comparative comfort of his shack.

CHAPTER THIRTEEN

— The Black Cat —

Lafitte's old fort straddled the narrow waist of the island, commanding the approaches to Spanish Cove. The square, thick walls, built to withstand all but the heaviest shelling, had bowed to time and weather. Cracks had appeared in the masonry walls, green vines had crawled up and around the ten-foot-high barrier, and corrosion had pitted the muzzles of the six pounders still in their emplacements.

Inside the walls was the masonry house. Time and vandals had taken their toll, so that only the big central room was still livable. LeCoste had fixed it up with rugs and some sticks of furniture, and off the big room was his shop and the small kilns where he baked his items of pottery and small clay animals.

The second squall, blowing up fast, had hit the island before he was ready to go back to the mainland. The squall and Carl Drake's brother, now lying on a cot by the far wall.

Now Jules brooded by the fireplace, watching thirty years of his life go by, leaving as little trace as the licking flames that disappeared up the flue.

He had waited a long time—perhaps too long. He clenched his bony fist tight on the head of his cane, staring at the dry, flaky skin and the pattern of pale blue veins below his knuckles. He was seeing for the first time the signs of age he had not been willing to concede.

Well, he had paid his price for Carlotta's jewels—he and Therese. What years were left to them it would be their right to enjoy. There was beautiful Paris and old Marseilles—cities where he and Therese would be at home. He had the money now to live as he had always dreamed of living.

He glanced at the girl sitting by the cot under the high bleak window. A waif, picked up by Therese—they owed her nothing. Yet she was pretty, he thought, as Therese had been thirty years ago.

It was a shame, he reflected gravely, that she had gotten herself involved with this man. . . .

Justine was crouched on the floor, watching Remington Drake's feverish face. . . . She had done what she could for him, but she knew, with frightened conviction, that he would be dead before morning. The youngster was still unconscious. Etienne's knife had dug deep. She had stopped the bleeding, but she could do little for the fever that was drying his lips or the infection that was beginning to take over around the raw, ugly wound.

Without medical help Remington Drake had little chance to live.

She knew this as she sat and watched the youngster's still white face. And she knew that Jules LeCoste had no intention of getting a doctor for Drake. Nor was she sure that she herself would live to see another day.

A black ironwood table, a relic of Lafitte's day, dominated the big room. Round and squat and incredibly heavy, it seemed as eternal as the rough stone walls.

The black jade cat sat alone on the giant pedestal, an insignificant, uncaring bit of pottery with its tail curled around its legs and an enigmatic smirk frozen forever on its tiny feline face.

Yet that bit of clay was worth more than ninety thousand dollars!

Etienne, squatting on his heels by the fireplace, looked at LeCoste. He was like some big watchdog, listening to the wind, to the far off noises in the violent squall.

His devotion was absolute. The relationship was that of lord and master, but the distinction was tenuous—there was more of a kinship between them. Etienne had been a soldier in Maximilian's Army, under LeCoste's command, and had come north with Jules after the collapse of the mad Emperor. To Etienne, home was where Jules LeCoste went. . . . Now he looked up at the old man, waiting for a break in Jules' thoughts, knowing how LeCoste hated to be disturbed. Finally he said: "The wind will be at our backs if we leave now. We could make the mainland before it gets too rough for safe crossing, Jules!"

LeCoste did not stir. He said: "We'll wait, Etienne. I am in no hurry."

He knew Myles Hegstrom would wait. No matter what he had told Jenkins, the trail boss would wait. There was too much money involved in this last delivery. Despite Myles Hegstrom's very real fear of the Ranger Riatt, he would wait. Greed, he reflected, was a powerful force.

Etienne suddenly came to his feet, his face turned to the door. The big black was frowning, listening to the beat of the rain, to the pounding of the waves on the seaward shore.

"I go see," he said finally. His bare feet padded softly as he headed for the door, then disappeared.

LeCoste followed the big black with his eyes. What had Etienne heard in the storm? The big black was like some jungle cat when it came to sensing things. . . .

Had someone been fool enough to cross from Lafitte in the howling squall? He smiled coldly, thinking of the Ranger known as Luke Riatt. Gosh Jenkins would have made his arrangements by now—and he felt a brief stir of curiosity as to why the powerful constable had been so insistent on taking care of the Ranger personally.

Jules LeCoste got up and turned to the table and stared at the black cat. The log flames flickered over the glazed surface, reflected dully from the green jade eyes. The smirk seemed to grow mysterious as he looked, and the eyes took on a solemn watchfulness.

Five men had died because of the cat—and more would follow! He turned his head and eyed the wounded man on the cot, his eyes devoid of sympathy. He had wasted too much of his own life to have qualms over taking of the lives of others.

Better to take care of him—and Justine—now.

Outside, the rain swept like a gray gauze sheet across the island spit. Riatt came up alongside the boat Drake had beached, jumped out and hauled it in to secure its position out of the water.

He was soaked clear through, but the exertion of bucking the wind warmed him. He moved with the easy grace of a stalking wolf. He followed the beach line to the jetty, briefly eyed the small boat moored on the calmer side. Jules LeCoste was still there, he thought grimly, and that meant the big black was also on the island.

He peered through the driving rain toward the old fort. Visibility was poor. All he could make out were crumbling battlements half smothered in masses of crawling vines. He could see no light, no indication of life. But he sensed it—somewhere in that pile of ancient rock were LeCoste and the girl, and Remington Drake, if he was still alive.

He moved slowly toward the ruins, rubbing the palm of his hand across the inner side of his leg to dry it. He might need a quick firm grasp on his Colt if that big black was on the prowl.

The squall ebbed with dramatic suddenness. One moment it was howling murderously; the next the wind had passed on to batter the town across the cove, leaving behind a fine mist rain to settle softly over the ruins of Lafitte's fort.

And that was when he heard it—the soft crack of a twig being stepped on! He heard it and was alerted, although he gave no indication of hearing. He was coming up an old, rain-slick path to what seemed a door in the ruins; the sound came from behind him.

He felt the hair on his neck prickle at the cold sensation of Death. Yet he held himself, his ears alert for another sound. If he turned now and it proved too soon, he could lose the man. . . .

It was fifty feet to that thick, bronze-hinged oak door. The muscles in his back crawled as he walked, tensing involuntarily against the bullet that could come, of the sharp, burning thrust of a knife. He walked those fifty feet like a man going to the gallows. . . .

He was at the door when he heard what he had been waiting for—the soft, quick pad of bare feet on wet earth, coming up fast!

Now he whirled, his gun hand coming up in a savage blur, his Colt glinting in the steel gray of the stormy sky. He had a glimpse of Etienne less than fifteen feet away, on the path, stopping abruptly, his right hand pulled back in the act of throwing a long-bladed, murderous knife!

Luke fired twice, both shots slamming into Etienne's hard stomach, tearing through him, doubling him. The knife arced wearily through the air, its force spent, and landed at Luke's feet. Etienne fell face forward, tried to crawl toward Luke, but went limp. . . .

CHAPTER FOURTEEN

— End Of The Trail —

Jules LeCoste heard the shots as he stopped by Justine's side. He had his silver-headed cane in his hand, the wicked blade sheathed in it half drawn. His eyes centered thoughtfully on the girl. Justine had risen slowly to her feet, the blood draining from her face. . . .

"You would kill us?" she whispered. "In cold blood?" And as she whispered the words she knew he would—this man she had called "Uncle."

Remington Drake's eyes opened. He looked up at her, then rolled his head to Jules. His mouth tightened grimly and he tried to get up —and that was when the shots that killed Etienne sounded outside, like flat firecrackers going off.

LeCoste whirled and backed away slightly. His eyes tried to bore through the closed door, as if he wanted to see through it. It could not have been Etienne who had fired; the big black had left without a gun!

The squall that had rocked and slammed at the old windows had subsided; in the quiet the drip, drip of water was now loud and clear. The sharp snap of wood in the fireplace alerted him. He had to know!

"Etienne!" he called. "Etienne!"

Behind him Remington Drake tried to get to his feet. He rolled off the cot, fell heavily. And Justine screamed!

LeCoste whirled toward her, his blade sliding free. He glided to her just as the door burst open at the impact of Luke's boot. A rush of wind came into the big room, fluttering the fireplace flames, fluttering LeCoste's eyes. He turned, pulling Justine before him; the point of his sword hovered at the base of her neck.

Luke Riatt was framed in the doorway, a Colt in his hand. He froze as he saw them, a big, wet, savage figure of a man who would not be denied.

Jules stood rigid, eyeing the big Ranger. From where he stood with Justine, he could see the bruises on the man's face, the raw welts on his throat. Gosh Jenkins had made a good try, he thought bleakly, but it had not been enough.

For the first time in his life fear made a raw track in his throat. He had come this far, this close to his dreams—he would not be stopped now.

"The gun, Ranger!" he whispered harshly. "Throw it here! Or—"

He pressed the point lightly against Justine's throat. . . . She quivered, her eyes wide and filled with fear.

Luke Riatt hesitated. The girl looked at him,

asking nothing; behind her, on the floor, Drake stirred.

"The gun!" LeCoste snarled. "Or would you prefer to see her die here!"

Luke Raitt drew a deep, harsh breath. He tossed the gun toward the old man, skidding it across the stone floor. It went past Jules, toward the cot—toward Remington Drake.

Jules turned to get it, and Justine broke away from him, flinging herself aside. And Luke made a run for the old man.

LeCoste wasted a moment looking for the gun, but Drake had fallen over it, trying to pick it up. He heard Luke coming and whirled back, the blade glinting in his fist.

Bat with a sword! That was what he looked like, with the cape flowing behind him. Tully's words came back to Luke Riatt.

He stood seemingly weaponless, helpless, as LeCoste lunged at him, and it was Jules' undoing. At the last moment he sidestepped, his hand flicking to his belt, drawing Etienne's knife. He drove it, swordsman style, into LeCoste's body as the man lunged past.

He felt the weight of the man against his fist. Jules' eyes went wide, staring, looking past Luke toward the door of his life—to the dark pit of death. His sword fell to the stone floor, clattering. When Luke withdrew his arm Jules folded slowly and fell on it.

Luke stood still, looking down at the dead old man. . . . Then he raised his eyes to Justine, in a corner, hand to her mouth, stifling a scream that was never uttered. She walked slowly to join him now and looked down on Jules. There was a momentary sadness in her eyes.

"He wanted the money so much—the money from the jewels!" she whispered. "For him and for Therese." She sighed. "Money and jewels that did not belong to them—that belong to France."

Behind her Drake was clawing to his hands and knees. She turned to him now, remembering and sharply concerned. She helped him to a sitting position on the cot, then turned to Riatt.

"Etienne did this to him. A bad cut, *monsieur.* He will die if he is not taken at once to a doctor!"

Luke nodded. "We'll get him there!"

He walked to Drake, bent and lifted him to his shoulder, fireman style. Justine walked with him. Luke paused on the way out to pick up his Colt, jam it into his holster. As they passed the heavy table he gestured to the small clay figure grinning at them.

"The cat," he said to Justine. "Take it with us!"

They went out into the fine mist sifting over the island, to the left the waves scraped the beach. They took Jules LeCoste's boat. Justine sat in the bow, with Drake's head pillowed in her lap.

The wind was behind them, driving them toward the mist-shrouded town of Lafitte. The waves were choppy, slapping hard against the skiff. Luke bent to the oars. The salt tang was in his nostrils; his wet shirt clung to his broad shoulders. The boat heaved up and down, nosing into the chop, and despite all the discomfort he liked it. This was the sea—the sea he had never seen until now.

They tied up at the pier where Luke had hired the boat. The man in the shack helped him with Drake; they took the wounded youngster to the doctor's house up on the hill.

Luke didn't stay. Outside, it was growing dark, and the rain still rode the wind in off the far reaches of the sea.

"I've got one last call to make, Justine," he told her. "Tell him, when he comes to, that I squared things for his brother."

Justine nodded. "I'll tell him!"

Myles Hegstrom waited impatiently at his camp by French Creek. The rain was a thin mist settling like a gray clammy covering over the camp. A hundred yards away the creek was flowing full and strong between its banks.

A big tarp, anchored at one end to the top of the chuck wagon and to stakes on the other, provided cover from the passing storm. Hegstrom and his men waited here, a small campfire providing light and heat for the big coffeepot.

The Open A boss sipped his coffee and eyed the faint trail to town. Night had come early, bringing with it a sense of foreboding. He had expected Jenkins before this. He didn't like the waiting, and it wasn't money that kept him there. He had salted away enough, from the other excursions, to put him beyond that need.

But fear of Jenkins' threat was real. He knew the big man well enough to know that his threat to come after him was not idle talk.

Still, there was a point beyond which he would not wait. His men, idle in camp, were getting restless; he did not want any of them to suspect why he remained there.

He had made arrangements for the burial of Tully and Slim; he had received payment for the cattle he had run into Lafitte's loading pens. There was no reason, according to the thinking of these men watching him, for him to stay there.

Frank Moss, an old hand with Hegstrom, ducked in under the tarp. Fine rain made tiny, jeweled beads on the brim of his hat, on his roan mustache. He jerked a thumb toward the road.

"Rider comin', Myles."

The Open A boss took a long breath. About time, he thought, and relief drew a pattern across his face. He got to his feet and walked to the edge of the covering and peered out into the night. He could hear the rider plainly now, but could not make him out; still, as the rider drew closer, a sudden fear tensed him. It wasn't Jenkins! He was too small, rode too easily. . . .

He picked up the rifle he had propped nearby and turned to face the man just coming into the firelight. Sam pulled up abruptly, freezing at the sight of that glinting muzzle.

"No need of that, Mister Hegstrom!" Sam's voice was quick, worried. "You remember me —in the Fortune Wheel?" As Hegstrom said nothing: "I worked for Jen—" He caught himself in time— "for Madame Paquet."

"You were right the first time," Hegstrom said coldly. "I know the Fortune Wheel belongs to Gosh Jenkins." He glanced past Sam, down the dark, empty road. "Where is Gosh?"

Sam glanced from Hegstrom to the men behind him, watching. He waited for a moment before replying. "Dead," he said solemnly. "That big feller—the one who called himself Smith—killed him!"

Hegstrom stood very still, feeling cold fear slide down into the pit of his stomach.

"Where's Smith?" The question came out of him, slow and bitter.

Sam shrugged. "Last I saw of him he was in a boat, rowing across the cove toward Jules LeCoste's place."

He dismounted, letting his horse stand in the fine rain, and walked toward Hegstrom. He said: "Mind if I have a talk with you alone?"

Hegstrom nodded. He turned and looked at Frank. "Get the wagons hitched up, Frank; round up the rest of the men. We're breaking camp and going home!"

Frank nodded and turned away. The others followed him, each man heading to saddle up, to stow away blanket rolls and gear.

Sam walked to the fire, picked up an empty coffee cup; he rinsed it out in the water bucket, poured himself a cup. He was very casual about it, very sure of himself.

Hegstrom eyed him with a slight frown. "Thanks for the information," he said shortly. "Now, if you'll excuse me, I'm going—"

"Not just yet, Mister Hegstrom," Sam said. "There's something else I came for."

He chuckled softly as Hegstrom stared at him. "Won't cost you much—not anywhere near as much as that black cat you came for!"

Hegstrom's voice was thick. "What are you talking about?"

"Five thousand dollars," Sam said. "To keep my mouth shut!"

He took a sip of his coffee, his good eye watching Myles, letting him sweat. "I know what was in that black cat," he said finally. "The customs people would like to know, too, eh, Myles?"

Around him the sound of his men breaking camp mingled with the slow crackling of the fire. Myles took a deep breath. "And if I pay you off—?" he began.

"I'll forget everything I know." Sam chuckled. "Won't be hard to do. I'll be in Vera Cruz, looking up a coupla old Fortune Wheel girls I know."

Myles made a motion to the wagon. "Got the money in there," he said slowly. "I'll get it!"

Sam nodded. It had been easier than he had figured. He took a long swallow of hot coffee, letting his thoughts drift on ahead of him, to Vera Cruz, to—

He turned quickly as Myles, at the back of the wagon, swung around to face him. "How much, Sam?"

"Five thou—" Sam started to say.

The bullet hit him up high, just under the level of the cup raised to his lips. It tore through his neck, below the bulge of his Adam's apple. The second bullet hit him in the back as he turned and was falling. . . .

Myles walked up to him, the small pistol in his hand still leaking smoke. Frank and some of his riders came running up; they stopped when they saw Sam.

Myles made a quick gesture to them. "Came in with a phony story about Jenkins; used it as an excuse to try to rob me." He slanted a hard look at Frank. "You and Flint take him to the river and toss him in."

Frank hesitated a moment.

"You want to stay here another two or three weeks, answering questions?"

Frank shook his head. He gestured to Flint; they picked Sam's body up off the ground and headed for the river. . . .

The wagons were hitched up and ready to roll. Frank and the remaining four Open A riders were mounted, flanking the lead wagon.

Myles walked to his saddled horse, held by Frank; he thrust his rifle into the saddle boot, looked up at Frank.

"Last time we'll be driving to Lafitte," he said coldly. "Any of you boys want to be paid off in the morning, speak up now."

The mounted riders stared at him. Frank said quietly: "You through with us?"

Myles shrugged. "I'm selling the ranch soon as I get back. . . ."

He shrugged at the look in Frank's eyes. "Time I got out of this business, Frank," he said harshly. "I—"

The voice came from behind him, cutting hard and cold. "Myles!"

Myles Hegstrom jerked around to face Luke as the big Ranger rode quietly out of the night.

166

A bitter regret welled up like gall in his throat. *He had waited too long!*

Luke eyed the mounted men behind Hegstrom, then laid his cold gaze on the Open A boss. "Leaving?" he murmured.

Hegstrom shrugged, hoping to bluff it out. How much did this big Ranger know? *How much?*

He forced a smile on his face. "Glad you showed up, Smith. Your job's open, but I didn't know if you still wanted it."

"The name's Riatt," Luke corrected coldly. "Luke Riatt—Texas Ranger!"

He saw the surprised reaction of the mounted men. Innocent men, he judged, whose only guilt was loyalty to a crooked boss.

Hegstrom smiled weakly. "Texas Ranger. You sure had me fooled—"

"Not really," Luke said coldly. He added dryly: "I've got the black cat, and a confession from Lolita. And I think Therese will talk now that Jules LeCoste is dead."

A small hammer of panic beat in Hegstrom's brain. Everything he had gained in four years was slipping through his fingers. . . .

He eased back against his saddled horse, feeling the stock of his rifle press against his shoulder. He said harshly: "I don't know what you're talking about. And—" for the benefit of his men —"I'm not even sure you are a Texas Ranger—"

"I'll prove it to you later," Luke cut in humorlessly. "Now get up on that horse. I'm taking you back to Lafitte!"

Myles took a deep breath. "All right," he said sullenly. He turned and put his hand up to the pommel. His eyes met Frank's, and he made a slight gesture with his head.

Frank kneed his animal away and made a grab for his Colt. . . .

Luke drew and shot him, aiming high deliberately. The bullet knocked Frank out of his saddle.

Hegstrom's fingers closed around the stock of his Winchester; he pulled it free and whirled on Luke, going into a crouch just as Riatt's slug hit him. He pumped one shot at the big Ranger, tried to work the lever for another shot. Luke's second shot killed him.

Luke's pivoting gun muzzle held the other mounted punchers rigid. Luke dismounted and walked slowly to Myles; the man was beyond help. He turned to Frank, who was sitting up, stifling a groan between clenched teeth.

"You'll live," he said coldly. Turning to the others, he made a short motion with his gun. "It's been a long wet ride, boys, and I'm banking for a cup of coffee. So let's get down and make camp again, eh?" His grin was cold and commanding. "I've got a few things to tell all of you!"

• • •

The morning sky was a bright blue, washed clean by yesterday's driving rain. The early sun beat against the front of the Fortune Wheel, across the windows whose drawn shades emphasized the blunt lettering nailed across the door:

CLOSED

Luke rode slowly to The Pierre House and dismounted. The sun was warm on his back; he worked his shoulders slightly to ease the stiffness in them.

Justine opened the door for him in Remington Drake's room. She was glad to see him.

"He is better," she breathed. "Much better. The doctor—"

"Come in, Luke," Drake called. He was raised on his elbow, propped up in bed, his chest and shoulders swathed in bandages. But his eyes were bright.

"Can't stay," Luke said gravely. "Three's a crowd." He looked at Justine, smiled. "I dropped by to say goodbye."

Drake nodded. "Will you be seeing Ann—my brother's wife?"

Luke nodded. "I don't think she ever believed Jenkins' story, but I think she'll be glad to read Lolita's confession." He walked up to the bed and gently knuckled Drake's jaw. "Remember to keep that chin up, kid."

Drake grinned weakly. "See you sometime, Luke."

He turned to look at Justine after the big Ranger had gone. His brother Carl had had the right idea when he had settled for Ann and kids, he thought.

Justine was looking out of the window. He called to her and she turned, her eyes soft, the bitterness gone from them.

"Will we see him again, some day?"

Remington Drake shrugged. "Some day. . . ." He held out his hand and she went to him. His arm went up to her, pulling her down to him, to a long and satisfying kiss, holding the promise of a bright future.

Center Point Publishing
600 Brooks Road ● PO Box 1
Thorndike ME 04986-0001 USA

(207) 568-3717

US & Canada:
1 800 929-9108
www.centerpointlargeprint.com